HINDSIGHT

Jack Howard

Printed in the United States of America

First Printing, 2015

ISBN 978-0-9964710-0-8

Cover art by Jeremy McQueen

For Sonia, my relentless sounding board and my closest friend.

<u>Chapter 1</u>

Bill Stratton sat in the pre-dawn darkness and shivered. The air was so cold it seemed to have frozen the world. On this moonless morning, the sole evidence of a horizon was a dim red line in the east, heralding the approach of the sun. The only sounds were the occasional stirring of rodents in the dry underbrush and the infrequent calls of quail in the distance. Bill opened an old thermos and drank from it. The dregs of mint tea were barely warmer than the still air. He replaced the lid and set the thermos aside, then stood up to stretch. Hunched slightly to avoid hitting his head on the wooden ceiling, he walked around the crude but well-hidden observation post, trying to warm up a little before his shift ended. On cold mornings such as this one, his limp was more pronounced. His simple clothing consisted of a shirt and pants made from doe-skin along with rabbit-hide boots, and he was wrapped in a cougar-skin blanket that barely covered his lanky frame.

He thought longingly of his warm cot with its buffalo-hide covers and said to himself, "Only a little while more."

The outpost was set into the top of a hill overlooking a makeshift settlement of about fifty refugees. This land was once known as South Texas, and was still called that by the elders. The rolling hills and heavy brush were full of thorny plants and venomous critters. But they also contained enough game to feed those who knew how to shoot or catch it, and the soil was fertile enough to grow some crops if the weather cooperated. The radiation had not poisoned the land here as much as it had further north where the plants grew short and twisted and the animals grew large and often asymmetrically deformed. Experience had taught him they were useless for anything but target practice. He had watched others try to eat them, and it often meant a slow and agonizing death for those poor hungry souls. The old-timers who had survived the fiery war and the long winter afterward had come south and managed to exist off the land after supplies from the "before-time," as many called it, ran out. Many of those people had been irradiated and died within months of the war, but enough had continued on as well. The small towns grew and then shrank, and some of them disappeared completely as their occupants moved on, doing whatever it took to survive.

Bill had been born in one of these settlements shortly after the war. He had grown up never knowing his father, but learning skills of survival from his very capable mother, Mary. She had been raised on a farm before the war, and her parents had taught her many of the old ways. *Thank God.* It was because of this teaching that Bill was still alive, and because he taught these skills to the others, he had become a valuable asset to the village below. Many of the townsfolk owed him their very lives. But he was getting on in years and wondered how much longer it would be before he stopped being useful and began to be a burden. He knew he'd end himself if that ever started happening—if someone else didn't do it for him first.

Looking out over the mostly darkened settlement, he breathed a shaky sigh. *And how much longer would these people survive?* It seemed the end of mankind was looming menacingly on the still barely visible horizon, just as dim and foreboding. It was lurching closer every day, and he felt helpless to stop it.

Bandits, the reason for this outpost and the constant watch, were roaming the countryside and stealing what others had worked so hard to build for themselves. They were killed on sight, at least if you could see them first. But many times they were too numerous to fend off, and so they took the food, the shelter, and eventually the lives of the prisoners they captured. They sometimes fought over the women and killed each other in the process. Cannibalism had become commonplace in these desperate times. The few survivors of these attacks, such as Bill, had told the stories. The bandits had taken from him his family and his reason for living, although he couldn't for the life of him remember the details of that horrible day, try as he may. The only thing that drove him now was his need to destroy the bandits and to help the good people, like the ones who slumbered in the settlement below.

As he looked out of the hidden post, the only source of light he could see other than the eastern horizon and the fading stars was the single fire that was kept burning constantly in the center of the small town, near the well pump. It was the meeting place, the cooking place, and the eating place for the people of the village. From its light, he could see the makeshift walls of the town, which had been constructed by stacking old cars end to end to a height of about twelve feet. The now useless crane used to build the wall lay in the darkness to the south, rusting in the brush. He could also see the ramshackle buildings made from whatever material could be scavenged from the nearby desolate towns. Those once-prosperous communities had become nothing more than deathtraps at night, often populated with hiding bandits waiting for some ignorant passing soul to come wandering through. Improvised towns with walls, like the one below him, were the best chance of survival. Crops could be grown nearby, and the animals they attracted could be trapped and eaten as well. As he looked at the shacks in the firelight, some of them had wisps of smoke coming from stovepipes on their roofs. It looked about as peaceful as it had almost every other night in recent weeks, but he knew better than to be lulled into a false sense of security.

Bill could also see that the other two watchmen were warming up next to the fire and talking instead of sitting at their posts on the wall. There hadn't been any sign of the bandits for a while, and they were getting a little too relaxed for his taste, but they were good men. He recognized them from the way they stood and gestured as they talked. On the right was David Lopez, who was about shoulder height to Bill but was also strong and about the best man he knew to have next to you in a fight. He was as close to being a friend as Bill would allow. The other watchman was Pete Downey, who was taller than Bill's six-foot height by five inches, and twice as wide with bulging muscles. His heart was just as big, but unfortunately he had the mind of a child. It didn't stop him from being deadly with a rifle though, and he was as good a watchman as the town had. They each carried firearms as did Bill, the three of which comprised the town's entire arsenal. They all knew how precious each cartridge was and used them sparingly.

As Bill watched the men, something flashed in his peripheral vision to the right. He turned to look and suddenly tensed. A light. He had not seen artificial light since his childhood, but he knew this was no oil lamp. It was bright white and moving fast. The light was still a few miles away, traveling on the old road, which was something once called a highway but was now mostly a pavement and dirt path where the brush wouldn't grow as big. This one led right to the gates of the town. He fumbled in the dark and found the old binoculars stored on the shelf under the main view port. With them he could see that the light was actually three lights, evenly spaced and set about four feet above the ground. He could see reflections on the grass and brush in front of what must have been a fast-moving truck. As a child, he had been allowed to ride in such a vehicle once, and it had both frightened and thrilled him at the same time. From the backwash of the bright lights, he could see huge wheels crushing the shorter brush with little effort. He looked back at the two watchmen, who were still by the fire. He needed to light the signal lamp. The truck was distant enough that it was still silent as he fumbled with the homemade matches. The first one wouldn't light after several strikes, and he threw it aside with a frustrated curse. The second one flared to life and he lit the wick, lowering the cover that allowed light to escape in only one direction. He aimed the feeble beam toward the watchmen.

"C'mon boys…look up here," he urged quietly with his soft southern drawl, but they were deep in conversation about who knew what. He glanced again at the lights. They were steadily moving closer.

David was the first to see the yellow signal lamp flame against the darkened hill, and he pointed at it. Both he and Pete raced for the wall and scampered up to their posts.

Once again David was first to see the approaching light, and he practically jumped from the wall as he ran to a bell mounted on a post near the fire.

He began ringing it loudly and yelling, *"To arms! To arms!"* The quiet settlement quickly exploded into activity as people emerged carrying pitchforks, shovels, clubs, spears, or whatever else they had handy. Some had homemade bows with arrows in quivers slung over their backs. They all raced to their pre-assigned places along the wall and peered through the gaps between the rusty vehicles, just as they had been taught to do when bandit attacks were imminent. The excitement was as thick as the anticipation and, though most of them had been asleep only moments before, they were ready for just about anything.

Chapter 2

It was still too dark to see much, but the entire eastern sky was beginning to glow pink. Bill could now barely hear the vehicle moving through the brush as the huge wheels crackled over mesquite shrubs and prickly pear cactus, their thorns squealing along its metal hull. Other than that it seemed to be silent, without the rumble of an engine he had heard on that first truck ride. It was still following the road and was about a mile from the village now. There was barely enough light to see that the vehicle was darker than the surrounding scrub and had strange sides, with a sharp edge and angles that sloped away on the top and bottom from a bulging center line. Bill watched it through the binoculars as it slowed some to cross a shallow wash, and then picked up speed on the nearer side. The lack of any mechanical engine sound was eerie and seemed somehow to make the morning air colder. Perhaps it was because of the crisp way the small branches were snapping louder now under the enormous tires. In the increasing light, he could see there were four of these wheels on the wide and long vehicle, just like most from the old times, but that was where the similarities ended. There was also a three-foot-wide dome on the top made of some shiny material that caught the glint of the brightening eastern sky. Looking for glass windows in the front, he found none—only more dark angled plates. He reached for his sniper rifle leaning against the wall next to the window and checked to make sure a shell was chambered. He set the binoculars aside and began watching through the rifle's large scope.

* * *

On the wall in his post next to the main gate, David was watching with another pair of binoculars.

He was loudly relaying information to the others as soon as he saw anything new. "Three lights, evenly spaced, about four or five feet off the ground, moving fast. Bandits must have gotten an old truck running." As the vehicle came closer, however, he realized there was no engine noise and said, "Hold up…something's different…I don't think that's a truck!"

Bob Earley, the town's oldest man and their accepted leader, was now in the post on the opposite side of the gate. "What the hell is it?" he asked.

"I'm not sure, but if it was a truck we'd hear the engine by now, right?"

Bob listened and thought for a moment. "Yeah, I can hear it moving through the brush, but nothing else."

Everyone was quiet and watching the two men or the brush. Even Pete, who loved to talk, waited in quiet apprehension at his post. The vehicle was slowing down as it got nearer, and when it was about 100 yards from the town gate, it stopped in the road.

David said in a quieter voice, "It stopped."

Someone along the wall who couldn't see the vehicle yelled, "What's it doing?"

David put his hand out to the voice without looking around and said quietly but urgently, "Shhhhh! It's just sitting there."

The vehicle sat with its lights still burning, facing the village. The deafening quiet was broken by an audible electronic click. Then there was a sound the old townsfolk had not heard in a long time—that of an electrically amplified voice.

"Good people, please do not be frightened. We come in peace." Nobody said anything, but eyes were darting around trying to understand what was happening. The voice continued. "We also come bearing gifts and wish to help in your survival. We would like to communicate with someone personally. As a show of good faith, one of the occupants of this vehicle will now emerge unarmed. Please do not be alarmed and do not fire your weapons."

David, who was now crouched in his post and peering over the barrier with his rifle and scope trained on the vehicle, saw the right side of the vehicle quietly split open, up and down along a the seam where the two sloping plates met. In the early morning light, he could see that the bottom half of the door had steps. A figure dressed in a white jumpsuit slowly stepped out with his hands in the air. He stood patiently next to the vehicle and waited.

David thought for a moment and then stood up while lowering his rifle.

Bob said, "Get down you fool! What are you doing?!"

David stood there watching the scene before him, but nothing threatening was going on. He turned to Bob and said, "I'm pretty sure they're not bandits. And I think if these guys wanted to hurt us, they would have already." He motioned to Pete to come over while he climbed down.

He walked over to Bob's post and tossed up the rifle, then turned as Pete ran over. "I need you both to keep me covered...I'm going out."

Bob stared at him, astonished. "Damn it man, are you crazy?" But he did nothing to stop David as he approached the door in the wooden gate.

Pete was still standing there watching him, as always slow to react. Then suddenly he charged up the ladder of the gate post and said with a grin, "Good luck David! We got you covered!"

David stopped at the door and backed up so he could see Pete at his post. "Pete!"

"Yeah?" he said, looking down.

"Don't shoot unless they do something *really* threatening, okay?"

"Oh, okay David. You got it! But they better not harm one hair on your head!"

"Just take it easy. I really don't think they're here to hurt us."

* * *

From the outpost, Bill watched as much as he could through the rifle scope. He had heard the amplified voice in the still morning air, not quite believing it...yet. Still, it was pretty obvious this was no bandit vehicle, although it did have a menacing air about it, as if it were built for killing as well as transport. There were no visible weapons, but it was heavily armored. If bandits were behind the controls, they would have crashed the gate by now and would be killing and capturing the townsfolk. And then there was the man in the white suit who also appeared to be unarmed. Bill could take him if he tried anything. He heard a noise from the settlement and swung the rifle to the left to see what his people were doing. He saw David emerging from the door in the gate, unarmed.

"What the hell are you doing now?" he said quietly. He thought he knew, though—probably the same thing he would have done. As he watched David

7

walk toward the vehicle, he noticed a slight movement in the brush near the road.

* * *

As David walked, his senses were on high alert. He noticed the usual early sounds from the brushy land were now absent. On any normal day there would be birds calling, even on a cold morning such as this, and he knew their absence usually meant trouble. He dismissed it as a result of the presence of the vehicle and kept walking. His approach did not seem to surprise the white-suited man, who was now smiling in a friendly manner.

David stopped about thirty feet from the front of the vehicle and asked, "What do you want?" He was trying to sound confident, but his voice broke slightly on the last word.

"As we said before, we come in peace and bear gifts."

"We don't need anything."

"Ah, but I'm afraid you do." Then, lowering his voice to a hoarse whisper, he continued, "This very day the bandits are going to attack in great numbers." The friendly smile never left his face.

"How do you know? Are you working with them?"

"Oh, no! Quite the contrary. In fact, that's the main reason we're here: to help you fight them. You see," he indicated the vehicle, "this machine can do wonders along those lines. If you wouldn't mind coming closer, I can demonstrate for you."

David stood looking at the man, trying to decide if he *had* been a fool to come out here without a weapon.

Zzzzzzzzzzt, pop!

The hyper-sonic bullet cut the air above and between them and connected with something to David's left, about twenty feet out in the brush. They both turned to see a mist of blood in the air as the sound of a rifle shot came from the outpost up on the hill.

Zzzzzzzzzzt, pop!

This time it was behind David, and he dropped to the ground, now realizing what was going on. He glanced at the man in the white suit, who was crouching

8

and beckoning frantically for David to come forward to the sanctuary of the vehicle. David decided quickly this time and scrambled for the doorway as rifle fire erupted from the brush all around them. As he dove through the open door, he could hear bullets whining off the hull. The man in white jumped through afterward and hit a button on the wall that rapidly closed the door. David turned over on his back, and from his position on the floor he could see two other men seated in chairs, also dressed in white jumpsuits. They had a series of control panels and lit-up screens before them and were working the switches quickly but calmly.

The original man in white sat at a third control chair and said, "Battle mode three, deploying weapons."

David watched the men work, fascinated by the way they seemed to carry out this attack with practiced efficiency. The sound of the bullets hitting the vehicle was tremendous, but they showed only concentration on their controls. On a large screen in front of the original man in white, he saw what looked like a series of green blobs surrounded by many red blobs. There were also contours of the land, brush and buildings. The town itself was recognizable in a purple circle around the green blobs. It was the towns-folk. There was also a green blob in the outpost. The man had hit some controls, and a sharp white circle had appeared on the screen surrounding some of the red blobs.

A woman's voice could be heard over the bullet impacts and seemed to come from everywhere at once, "Commencing fire."

* * *

From his outpost on the hill, Bill continued firing at the bandits. The bastards had come during the night and were waiting for dawn to attack the town— about a hundred of them by the look of it. He had spotted them in the brush as David approached the vehicle and managed to pop the heads off two before all hell broke loose. A couple of bullets had come his way, but most were directed at the vehicle. He could see sparks jumping from its hull and then his friend diving inside. That's when everything changed.

The dome on top began to quickly extend, and soon it appeared to be a shiny silver ball on a large post. As it rose about ten feet above the vehicle and stopped, a loud hum began to fill the air. Suddenly a thin, bright-blue beam shot out of the ball and moved horizontally through the brush about ten feet from the left of the vehicle, then disappeared. Where it had connected with brush, there was fire and smoke. Then another beam appeared, moved, and disappeared, this time in another spot in the brush—then another. Soon it was happening very rapidly all around the vehicle, in an ever-widening circle. Bill watched in astonishment as the bandits began to run but were literally cut in half by the beam. The sound of gunfire was quickly replaced with the screams of the dying.

* * *

David heard the control panels beeping and saw the moving red blobs on the screen begin to flash brighter, one at a time, then fade. The beeping became faster and the bullets slowed. In less than a minute all the red blobs were gone. The bullets had stopped, and the only sound was the humming and whirring of the machine. The green blobs were all still there, including the one on the hill.

The female voice sounded again. "Firing terminated."

The original man in white said, "Expanding search…." He flipped some switches, and the screen view changed. There was no red in sight. "All clear."

He flipped one more switch, and the female voice sounded. "Stowing weapons."

David looked around at the three men. "What just happened?"

The man in white looked at him and said, "It's safe now. The battle is over. All the bandits are dead."

Chapter 3

Sixty-five miles to the southeast of this battleground, a large man sat alone in a room. He was cross-legged on a small pillow with a candle burning in front of him on the floor. He wore only a dark purple robe. Other than the pillow, the room was furnished with shelves containing dinner plates, vases, glasses, and other fine breakables. The man's eyes were closed and moving rapidly behind their lids under a protruding brow. He appeared to be asleep. He looked as if he had dreamed a very disturbing dream that had started out pleasant enough, but had turned very bad, very quickly indeed. The door to the room began to rattle a bit on its hinges as a deep rumbling sound seemed to come from the walls.

The man inhaled slowly.

He opened his eyes and began to scream in rage.

The candle fell over and went out.

* * *

Two hundred sixty-five miles to the northeast of the battle, another much smaller man sat alone in a room. This room was well lit with white walls but was not furnished at all. He was wearing a white jumpsuit. His pale, pink-gray skin was the only color in the room. The man sat on the floor, cross-legged as well, but his face held no expression. His large eyes were also closed but made no movements behind their lids.

After a short while, the small man's body began to rise a few inches above the floor.

Chapter 4

David was sitting on the floor of the vehicle looking at the three men in white.

"Who *are* you guys?"

They were shutting down the equipment, and it was becoming much quieter. It was quite warm inside, and when they opened the door again the cold air rushed in.

"Come. We'll talk in your camp. Call down the man from the hill. Everyone will want to be in on what we have to offer." The man who had greeted David earlier helped him stand up and step out of the vehicle.

"What is this thing?" he asked, once they were outside.

"It's a Mobile Armored Security System. We call it a MASS tank for short. Pretty impressive, don't you think?"

David looked at the carnage around him. There were small fires still burning in the sparse brush, and the smell of scorched flesh was strong in the air. Smoldering mounds of human remains were scattered everywhere.

"Yeah, impressive." He looked at the town gate and saw Bob and Pete looking at them. Even from this distance he could see they were both wearing expressions of utter disbelief. He waved to show that he was not hurt, and they turned to tell those who couldn't see through the holes in the wall.

The original man in white said, "My name is Samuel." He held out his hand to David, who shook it absently, still looking around at the dead bandits. "This is Joseph, and that is Curtis." They also shook hands. "You must be David."

David stopped looking around and stared at Samuel. "How do you know my name?"

"Come. Let's walk to your camp. We have much to discuss," Samuel said. The friendly smile was back on his face.

* * *

"As I said before, we come in peace and bear gifts," Samuel spoke to the group gathered in the middle of the town. Most were sitting as close to the fire as possible. The entire town listened, including Bill. A runner had been sent to retrieve him, but it wasn't necessary. He had already made his way, hobbling down the hill as David, Samuel, and Curtis were walking from the vehicle toward the village. Joseph had stayed behind with the MASS tank to keep watch in case any more bandits showed up.

"We know this is all new to you, but we have many vehicles like the one you saw this morning. Some of them are waiting a few miles from here and will approach when we give the signal. That is, if you want them to. We also have food and blankets. We even have toys for the children." He looked at some of the younger members of the group and smiled.

Bob was the first to speak up. "What do you want?"

"I'm sorry?"

"What do you want from us? You come here and kill all these bandits...tell us you have food and toys that you're going to give us. You must want something in return."

"Yes, as a matter of fact we do. But we'll get to that later. For now, if you give us permission, we'll call in the other tanks and let the feast begin."

"Now hold on." Bill stood up and looked at Samuel. "Before we agree to anything, we want to know what you expect us to give you." His glare told Samuel he would not bend on this.

"Okay, fair enough. Your name is Bill Stratton, correct?"

"Yes."

"Well, Bill, we have come for you."

Bill stared at him. "Me? And how the hell do you know our names, anyway. David here told me you knew his, too. You have to know all this makes us a little...uneasy."

"Of course, and for that we apologize. It is not our intention to offend, but we really do need your help, Bill. And for your services, we are willing to bring food, additional shelter and protection."

"Protection."

"Yes, in the form of three MASS vehicles, complete with operators. You saw what one could do, and we're leaving three. The bandits will never be a threat again. We also have a team who can teach you better farming methods. We even have seeds."

Bill thought about this for a moment. "Okay, I get that you guys are better than us—better at fighting." He looked out the now open gate at the tank. "Better at defense. So why do you need me?"

"We have a mission that requires someone with a very special skill set. Much like yours."

Bob had been watching this and felt the need to speak up again. "Now just a damn minute! Bill here is one of our best men. You can't just come in here and take him from us!"

"Oh, make no mistake, Bob, we're not going to take anyone." He turned back to Bill. "If you come with us it will be completely voluntarily. And as I said before, we are willing to leave ample protection for this village."

Once again, Bill thought about it. "You're going to have to do a lot more explaining before I know I can trust you. These are good people. You did a real good thing this morning. Those bandits…they probably would have killed us all. But I can tell you're not being completely straight with us."

"Yes, you're right. But there are many parts of this mission that must remain in secret…for now. I know how that sounds, but it really is necessary or it will all be for nothing. The mission will fail before it even gets started."

Bill walked around the campfire, his limp slightly better. The sun was above the wall now, and it felt warm on his face. He looked at the people who had taken him in when he was too broken to walk. They had helped him survive, and he had helped them.

"Listen, Bill," Samuel said, "if you say the word, we'll just leave. You can all go back to struggling like you were before."

Bill looked back at the vehicle through the gate. He turned to Bob. "Just one of those things out there took on a hundred bandits and wiped them out in seconds. That's something I could never do. And they want to leave three of 'em here. You'll be better off a thousand times over if I go with them. That's worth any risk."

Bob looked at the men in white and then back at Bill. "I guess you're right."

He looked around at the faces of the townsfolk and could tell they were as torn as he was. Then he looked out the gate at the piles of bandit remains. "But dagnabbit, Bill! Do you want to go? I mean put what's better for the town aside. What do *you* want to do?"

Bill thought for a moment while looking out at the tank in the roadway. Its sharp, sleek lines stood out against the brushy background, and its silver dome shone like a beacon with the reflected sun.

"Well, I reckon I'm kinda curious. If they're willin' to leave those things here to protect ya'll, I'm willin' to go find out why they need me so much."

Bob thought for a minute and finally he made the decision. "We're sure gonna miss you, Bill."

"Excellent!" Samuel smiled broadly. He turned to Curtis. "Tell the crew to come in and set up the feast!"

Curtis reached into his pocket and pulled out a small black box with a short metal rod sticking out of the top. He pressed a button on the side and spoke into the box, "Bring 'em in." The box emitted a tinny "Affirmative."

Bill looked at Samuel again. "What exactly is this mission of yours supposed to accomplish?"

"Why, Bill," Samuel said with a huge smile. "If I told you that, it'd spoil all the fun!"

Chapter 5

Craig Jones listened to the man in the room screaming and cringed. The dishes in the room were being smashed against the walls and floor. This was not good. When Craig had set up the room an hour before, Ramey, or "The Boss" as he demanded to be called, had been in such a good mood. He had only heard his master this angry on one other occasion, and on that day some of his friends had died as a result. He only hoped Ramey would not emerge from the room and kill the first person he spotted, as had happened on that terrible day.

Craig sat quietly at his desk, trying not to tremble. Nothing in the world scared him except his master, who was the only person he knew that was bigger than him. But it wasn't only his size that made him fear The Boss. It was the way he did things, especially when he was this angry. When he saw his friends die, Ramey hadn't even touched them. He just looked at them one by one, and they fell over dead. Just like that. He was lucky enough to have been behind the man, and so he didn't see the horrible look on his master's face—so terrible it made you die—but he had seen it on other, less consequential occasions. And he had felt its effects. Craig could kill any man with his fists, and had done so many times. But how could you fight a look that would end your life instantly?

The crashing continued in the next room, but the screaming had died down and was now a series of swears that would make even the hardest criminal blush. He remained at his desk only because The Boss had told him to before he went into the room. If it were up to him, he would run from the building and never stop, but he knew even that would be of no use. The Boss could find you no matter where you went. He could find anyone he wanted to…except his twin brother.

* * *

The small body of the man in the white room continued to float a few inches above the floor. It remained there, perfectly still, and could do so for hours or days if he wished it to. It required very little food or water when it was in this state because its functions had slowed to a pace that was the minimum required to keep it alive. That was because the man known as the "Traveler" wasn't there with his body.

Instead, he was two hundred sixty-five miles to the southwest, watching the feast in the small village. He saw the hungry townsfolk ravenously eating the turkey, deer, chicken, bread, and assorted vegetables his community had provided them. He saw them accepting the blankets, gardening tools, and seeds. He saw the children running and laughing with the toys. They had a little extra energy from the candy they had been given. He saw his crews piling the remains of the bandits into an excavated ditch some distance from the town and then covering them over with several feet of dirt. One of the MASS tanks had been modified for this, and another had been modified to put out the brush fires. The still-working firearms had also been gathered from the bandit bodies and brought into the town. Some of them had been destroyed by the beams. He saw three of the ten tanks he had sent take up triangular sentry positions, one of them on top of the hill where the sniper, Bill, had been when the first vehicle arrived.

He saw Samuel talking to the townsfolk about how crews would stay and man the three MASS tanks. Samuel explained how even the huge tires were filled with foam rubber, so scores of bullets wouldn't ever flatten them. He explained how the spherical LASER cannon worked under its bulletproof coating and how its thousands of lenses, as well as the MASS computers and strong electric engines, were powered by tiny but durable nuclear plants in each vehicle. Many of the men were duly impressed and nodded their heads knowingly, though most had no idea what he was talking about.

The Traveler had also watched the battle, during which he had noticed another disembodied presence. He could not see it, but he knew it was there. He recognized the familiar but menacing energy it exuded. He had known it all his life, even though he and his brother were separated at birth. The Traveler and his twin shared some of the same abilities, but that was where the similarities ended. The other presence had left shortly after the battle, but not before emitting a burst of hateful energy, unnoticed by everyone but The Traveler.

Chapter 6

After the feast and Samuel's briefing, Bill was taken aside to his hut and prepared for the trip. He still had many questions, but the crew politely informed him that they were not allowed to talk about it. They gave him a change of clothes—a white jumpsuit, of course—and a new pair of boots. They also gave him some toiletries and instructed him on how to use them. Apparently, he smelled bad to them. Bill hesitated, but finally doffed his old reliable skins and applied the cleansers. Then he put on the jumpsuit, which was remarkably comfortable and warm. He felt a little self-conscious as he emerged with the two crew members and heard some nearby children giggling. He smiled and made a face at them, which sent them into hysterics.

They walked to the town center where Bob was talking with Samuel. They were looking at Bill's sniper rifle on one of the eating tables that had been cleared by the women.

Samuel said, "That is one fine shooting instrument, and well-maintained." It was an old Army 30-06, used back in WWII by snipers in Europe. The scope had been upgraded with a more powerful model. It was an antique weapon, but still in perfect working order.

"Well," Bob replied, "It's no match to one of them tanks."

Samuel laughed, "Yeah, you have to admit, they're pretty impressive. Wouldn't you agree, Bill?"

Bill had approached and sat down next to Bob. "I suppose, but they look complicated. I like my weapons simple. Less likely to break down."

"Yes, that's true. We have had our difficulties. These machines are very new, but they are the best we have. We brought several of them, leaving our community partially unprotected. We do need to get going pretty soon."

"Now just a dad-gummed minute!" Bob said. "I still don't like this. Bill, you sure you want to go traipsing off with these people to God knows where?"

Bill was a generally quiet man who usually spoke only when it was necessary. He had a lot of experience with fighting bandits, and much of what he said since his arrival had been while teaching the townsfolk to fight. He looked at the men and then looked around at the town. Finally his gaze settled on Bob.

"When ya'll found me I was near death. You took me in and doctored me until I healed, and for that I am eternally grateful. I've tried to help ya'll learn to fight off these bandits since then, trying to repay what you did for me. But you saw what happened this morning. If these gentlemen hadn't showed up when they did with their fancy tanks, we'd all be dead or dyin' right now. Or worse, wishin' we'd never been born. Now, like I said before, I think if they're willin' to leave three of these tanks and a crew to run them, then the least I can do is go see what they want me to do for 'em." He looked at Samuel. "Only thing is, after what I saw this morning, I can't see what I could do that they couldn't."

"Well, sir," Samuel replied, "as I said before, you have a unique skill set. You proved that today, just at the beginning of the battle."

"What, poppin' those two? Your tank could've done that."

"Yes, but your skill with a rifle is only part of the mission plan. And please don't ask anything else about that. You will be briefed as necessary and full disclosure will eventually come. But it is of utmost importance that you don't know too much too early. And the reason for that must be kept from you as well, for now."

After a moment, Bill said, "All right, what's first."

"Excellent! First thing we have to do is get you to our community training center. The trip will be long, but comfortable. You'll be riding with me in the lead tank." He pulled the black box from a pocket in his jump suit. "Eddie, round up the crew and set up the convoy. We leave in twenty."

The box made an electronic click, and someone, supposedly Eddie, said, "Copy."

"Mr. Stratton, if you would like to say your goodbyes to the townsfolk, now is the time to do it."

"You don't mind if I take this with me do you?" Bill said as he stood and placed his hand on the rifle.

"Well, your people will still need it for hunting. These tanks can kill game, but they're messy at it. Don't worry, where you're going you won't need it."

Chapter 7

Craig was still sitting at his desk when The Boss emerged. He stood shakily, out of respect, but also braced himself for what would surely be his last moments on Earth. The noises coming from the room had subsided a few minutes earlier, and he assumed that meant his leader had run out of things to break.

"One hundred men." The Boss sounded remarkably calm, and Craig let out a quiet sigh of relief. "One hundred men and he killed them all."

"All of them? But how?" Craig's voice betrayed his efforts to appear composed.

"He has some new toys. Apparently he's been busy."

"Did they at least find out what the target was?"

"No, they didn't get the chance." The note of anger in The Boss' voice caused Craig to tense again. "They were too busy shooting at my brother's toys and getting killed. Buncha damned idiots."

Craig watched his leader in silence as he stood thinking. The Boss's already protruding brow seemed to jut a little further over his dark eyes. Finally he spoke.

"Has the alpha crew finished at the base?"

"No, sir. They had to go north for more parts."

"Damn it!" He punched his fist through a nearby wall and Craig winced. "Gather the crew leaders and send them to the conference room. Be quick about it!"

Craig exited the room as fast as he could and went to the communications office down the hall. He entered to see the operator lounging in his chair and reading an old comic book. It was in remarkably good condition.

"What the hell do you think you're doing?" The operator jumped up, spilling the cup of water on the TV tray next to him and soaking the other comic books he had found.

"Nothing, I—"

"Just get on the horn and gather the crew leaders. Send them to the conference room. ASAP!"

"Yes, sir!"

"And get rid of those books! You know how The Boss feels about reading."

"Absolutely, sir. Won't happen again."

"It better not, or I'll have your nuts in a sausage grinder."

Craig left without listening for a reply. He knew what was to be done next and headed for the cafeteria. The Boss liked food available at his meetings, not only to eat but to throw at his captive audience when he wanted to make a point.

He had a feeling a lot of people would be wearing chow today.

Chapter 8

As Russell approached his body, he began speeding up its functions again. He preferred being outside of it, but found it hard to control that way. His body was small and frail, but he could operate it very efficiently. He saw that it was levitating again, and as he inhabited it, he made it move and stretch as it settled down to the floor. It would be so easy to just leave it and go cavorting through the universe with so many interesting places to see. But he knew he needed it to help his people and this planet to survive. He couldn't just leave them in their current condition, especially at the mercy of his brother. He needed his body to control the environment around him. He could only do so much without it.

He stood up, once again feeling the effects of gravity, and went out the door of the white room. His bare feet made no sound as he padded down the hall. Ellen Schertz was waiting for him in the break room, drinking mint tea and eating a mesquite bean cookie. She was blond and petite, but a powerhouse of energy when the going got rough, and she made an excellent assistant.

"Everything went according to plan." Russell was standing in the doorway looking at her. His voice was pleasant to everyone who heard it. He was speaking telepathically, as he always did, and Ellen heard his voice in her head. "They should arrive sometime tomorrow."

"That's excellent, sir. Preparations are being made." Ellen smiled at him. No one else could speak without using their mouths, but Russell never held it against them or talked down to them. He was always pleasant, unless someone was trying to hurt his people. Ellen's smile broadened. "You look better."

"Yes, I find it invigorating to travel." He had been tired from the weeks of preparation for today's battle.

"And the special guest is unhurt?"

"Yes, he's fine. Even managed to get a few of my brother's minions before the MASS tank took care of the rest." Everyone in Russell's inner circle had been briefed extensively on today's activities, and the tank crews had trained thoroughly. They could afford to make no mistakes and were also trained to be flexible and to adapt to almost any contingency.

"Thanks to your good training," Ellen said. "The engineers will be happy to hear about the tanks. They are working hard and the Kronos should be ready for a test run soon."

"Very good. I want you to schedule a party for when they're finished. Plenty of food and some of Joe's special brew. They deserve it."

"Yes, sir." She smiled again. She sipped her tea in thought, and then her face became more serious. "Our guest—"

"Please, call him by his name."

"Okay—Bill—are you sure he's the right man?"

"Oh, yes. He has just the right background and skills." He gazed at her with concern. "It is unlike you to question my choices. Is everything all right?"

"Yes, sir. It's just the reports coming in from the scouts—everything's getting worse. I'm afraid to let Sarah go outside to get sun anymore. A lot is riding on this mission."

Russell knew her six-year-old daughter well and was quite fond of her. He also knew many of his own people had disappeared—all of them valued members of the community—and some had been taken in broad daylight. He sat down across from her.

"Ellen, you have every right to be worried. But we're doing everything we can to fix this. You know that. We're going to fix it, and then—things will be better. Failure is not an option. We will succeed, and your Sarah will be beautiful when she grows up. She will need to take self-defense classes to fight the boys off. Now, you go and make those arrangements for the celebration. And don't forget Joe's brew."

"Yes, sir." She thought about how the "brew," a beer made from fermented wheat, made the personnel rowdy. She smiled again and got up from the break room table, taking her tea with her.

"And Ellen, you're going to the party and you will enjoy yourself. You've been working hard as well."

Her smile managed to broaden even further.

Chapter 9

The ride in the MASS tank was much smoother than Bill thought it would be, and very quiet. This was much better than his ride in the truck so many years ago. He was strapped into a cushiony seat that swiveled around. There were no windows, but the screens gave a good view of the front, sides, and back of the tank. He recalled stories of TV sets and had seen the old useless boxes with glass screens among the rubble in the abandoned buildings. These were the first working picture screens he had ever experienced. He could see the line of tanks making their way through the brush behind them. The "auto-navigator," as they called it, was doing most of the driving. Two of the crew members were with him, Samuel and Curtis, the latter of which was sleeping soundly in his chair. Samuel sat in the main control chair but was only occasionally changing the view on the screens.

Without turning to Bill, he said, "I trust you said your good-byes to your satisfaction?"

Bill had gone to his closest companions one by one and told them he may not see them again—that he had no idea where he was going or what he'd be doing. He told David to take care of the townsfolk. David had replied that he had tried to get these strangers to let him come along, but they had told him it was imperative that only Bill go. They wouldn't consider any alternatives—said something about jeopardizing the mission. Bill told him it was better this way and that the town needed him. David's wife Leticia had wept openly and given him a long hug.

He looked at Samuel. "Yes. They're good people…. I hope you know that."

Samuel turned in his swivel chair to look at him. "Don't worry about them, they're in good hands. Here, look." He turned a knob to the number six and flipped a switch. The screen above the controls flickered and the view changed. Suddenly Bill was looking at the town from the hill with the observation post.

The sun was bright in the blue sky and he could see the burned areas in the brush from that morning's battle. Samuel manipulated the controls again and the view zoomed in on the center of the town. The children were still running around with their toys, and he could see Pete following Bob around and talking his ears off.

"You can check in on them any time you like. The signal will reach where we're going."

"Where is that exactly?"

"Okay. First of all, we need to swear you to secrecy."

"What?"

"I'm very serious. This mission cannot fail, and if you happen to talk to your friends," he indicated toward the screen, "and if something should happen and they were captured by the bandits...let's just say the less they know, the better it is for them. The leader of the bandits is evil in its purest form. He has no compassion and doesn't allow his followers to show any. And he would stop at nothing to find our leader. Do you understand?"

Bill thought about his past experience with the bandits and said, "Yeah, I think I do."

"All right. Please raise your right hand." Bill reluctantly complied, still thinking this was a little silly. "Repeat after me. I, William Stratton, do solemnly swear..."

"I, William Stratton, do solemnly swear..."

Bill repeated the promise to keep all information he took in to himself and not to divulge it to any unauthorized personnel even if he were tortured in the most unimaginable ways.

Samuel said, "Good. I trust you are a man of your word or The Traveler wouldn't have chosen you."

"Who?"

"The Traveler is what we call our leader, and you won't find a better one on this planet. He has...certain abilities—powerful abilities the rest of us don't have. Yet he is still as friendly and approachable as you could want. He has been watching you for some time."

"What? How?"

"In time, Bill. Right now you should get some sleep. I know you've been up all night on watch, and you must be exhausted."

"You tell me all this and you want me to sleep?"

"Yes. You should rest assured that all your questions *will* be answered."

Bill turned to look again at his home of the past few years on the screen. Pete was now following one of the crewmen walking out the gate toward a sentry tank, still talking at full speed. Just the thought of listening to Pete made him sleepy.

"All right, I'll try."

"You can recline your seat with a button on the side."

Bill looked down and saw the buttons clearly marked with diagrams of the seat in upright and reclined positions. He pushed the latter and the seat back began to move. He was a little startled when a leg rest also came up, but soon found the new position quite comfortable. Samuel had turned back to his controls. With his eyes closed, Bill was surprised how quickly sleep began to overtake him. His last thoughts were of the fine venison steak he had eaten at the feast, so tender and seasoned just right, and then relaxing darkness.

Chapter 10

"One hundred men!"

Ramey paced around the oval table where his crew leaders were seated. He was carrying a half-eaten and undercooked turkey leg, pausing now and then to take a bite, but not letting a full mouth slow down his rant.

"He killed all of them!"

The crew leaders sat in the conference room with full plates of food, but as yet none were eating. They watched The Boss silently until he met their eyes and then they looked down quickly, afraid of conveying the wrong message and receiving his infamous wrath.

"And he did it in seconds this time." Ramey bit into the drumstick again. "He's got some new toys with killer beams shooting out of the top." As the last word left his lips, so did a small piece of wet turkey meat. It landed on the bald head of a crew member, who flinched but dared not brush it away.

"They're armored. Rifle fire didn't seem to have any effect on 'em, but I don't think they'll be any match for our tanks, though. Smith! Progress report!"

Ed Smith was Ramey's head engineer and was in charge of refurbishing the hundreds of abandoned U.S. Army tanks left over from the war. They were scattered up and down the river, which used to be the border between Texas and Mexico, and were usually found rusted and useless. "We have twenty-two working tanks with seventeen more in various stages of repair. Estimated time to full repair is four weeks. Additionally we have roughly two thousand rounds of working ninety millimeter ammo for the big guns, and over three-hundred thousand rounds of armor-piercing ammo for the machine guns."

Ramey threw the remains of the drumstick at Smith, who took it in the chest, only flinching slightly. The leg bounced onto the table and was purposefully ignored by the crew leaders.

"Not good enough! I want all those tanks working in two weeks. And we need more ammo."

Smith was about to argue, but there was a sudden look of surprised horror on his face. He looked down at his plate instead and quietly said, "Yes, sir," sounding as if the wind were knocked out of him, "no problem."

"That's right. Jimenez, report!"

Hector Jimenez was The Boss's fuel specialist. "We've filled all the storage tanks to capacity as well as the tanks on the...um...tanks. Since we have nowhere else to store the fuel, we have slowed production temporarily at the plant. The power station will always need gasoline, as well as your personal transportation, of course."

"Well, finally! Somebody's doing something right." Ramey beamed his crooked yellow-toothed grin upon Jimenez, who allowed himself a slight smile as well. The Boss reached down to another crew leader's plate and picked up a piece of deer meat as he passed by. He took a bite of the tough steak and chewed thoughtfully as he strolled slowly around the room. The seated members shot jealous glances at Jimenez, who had wisely stopped smiling.

"If we can pull this together in two weeks," Ramey continued, "we just might crush my brother where he lives."

He took another bite of venison and turned to Craig, who was seated at the end of the table. "I want you to dispatch two of your best scouts. Tell them to give the town from this morning a wide berth to avoid enemy fire because I'm sure my brother left some of his toys there. But he was after somebody in that town, and he'll bring them back home. My brother's toys approached from the northeast. Tell them to pick up the tracks on the other side and give them the long-range radios so they can report their progress. This is a rare opportunity to find out where their headquarters is, so they better not screw it up!"

"Yes, sir," Craig said, "I was thinking the same thing. Johnson and Fernandez will be prepped and on the way within the hour."

"Good. Put them on horses...I don't want them to draw attention, but speed is important. Is that clear?"

"Crystal." Craig sat patiently while The Boss continued to pace.

"All right. I'm going to go get some real food. You can eat your slop now." He threw the rest of the deer steak onto the middle of the table and walked out the door.

A collective sigh of relief could be heard at the table. All eyes then turned to Craig, the second in command.

He looked around the table and said, "You guys have been around long enough to know that that went fairly well, especially after that attack fiasco this morning. The Boss is right, though. His brother doesn't make many mistakes, but he may have made a fatal one this time. If we can find the headquarters, we'll break him and his namby-pamby followers where they live. And they've obviously been living pretty good if they can make those weapons he described. We can take it all from them and then we'll be the ones living in comfort. Now eat quick and get back to work." He shot a sharp look at Ed, who was still looking down at his plate. "I'm going to go talk to the scouts." He grabbed his plate and walked out the door.

Immediately, most of the crew leaders tore into their food, which was a treat for them in these hungry times. Ed continued to stare at his plate for a while.

"I could feel it," he muttered. The others slowed down to stare at Ed. "I could feel him pushing me out again."

The members shot nervous glances at each other. They had all felt it at one time or another when The Boss's anger was directed their way. It was like an unstoppable force pushing you out of your body, and they all knew it was the way he killed with a look. He'd push you out and then stop your heart or something so you couldn't get back in. It was a very uncomfortable feeling that left one bewildered and nauseated. Ed sat staring at his food a few moments longer and then slowly stood to leave without eating. As soon as he had cleared the doorway, the members seated near his chair attacked his plate as well.

Chapter 11

Bill woke to the smell of food. He opened his eyes slowly and looked around without moving. The MASS tank was rocking gently as it traveled on the old road, and its interior lights were turned down low. The screens showed a dark landscape illuminated by the headlights and side lights unhurriedly rolling by. The air carried a tantalizing fragrance of stew. He was still strapped into the chair and hadn't seemed to have moved at all as he slept. As he raised his head to search for the source of the aroma, his neck felt stiff.

Curtis was in the control seat, and Samuel had moved to a station behind them and was sitting on a low bench, stirring a steaming pot on a ledge that popped out from one wall of the tank. The pot was spherical with a small opening at the top so it wouldn't spill in the rocking vehicle. The ledge was glowing red under it. Samuel glanced up to see Bill craning his neck to look at him.

"Ah, good morning! You must have been exhausted. You've been asleep for over ten hours."

Bill was visibly stunned. He hadn't slept that long in…well, he couldn't remember ever sleeping that long. He fumbled with the buttons and got the seat to go upright. With little effort, he swiveled it around to face Samuel.

After stifling a yawn and while rubbing his neck, he asked, "Where are we?"

"We're about two-thirds of the way home. Right now we're traveling south of what used to be a city called Houston. It got a light hit on its northwest side during the war. Almost all of the warheads targeted there overflew it and went into the countryside beyond. There was enough damage and radiation, however, to kill most of the people and make the city uninhabitable. A good deal of it still is."

He looked down at the pot. "I thought you might be hungry, so I'm warming up some of the rabbit stew from yesterday. I know I can use some."

"So, where is…home?"

"Ah, that's an interesting question." Samuel was smiling again. "The Traveler picked this site because it was equipped with certain items and buildings we need for the mission and because it's easy to hide from the bandits."

"Uh, if we're trying to hide from the bandits, aren't we leaving an awful big trail to your base? I mean," he indicated the rear-view screen, "those tracks could be followed by anybody, let alone a tracker, which I'm sure they're sending out."

Curtis said, "Don't worry. We're leaving one of these tanks behind in a strategic location. Any trackers will be in for a little surprise."

"We're not taking any chances on failing the mission," Samuel continued, still stirring the stew.

"The mission," Bill said, a little irritated.

"Yes, I know you still have many questions, but they will have to wait a little while more. You're a lucky man, Bill," Samuel smiled, "because today you're going to meet The Traveler."

Bill watched the landscape roll by in the view screens. "Lucky, huh? Can you at least tell me what I'm going to be doing on this mission?"

"Well, I can tell you it involves travel, but not in a MASS tank. You'll be in something a little less primitive."

"Less primitive? What's that supposed to mean?"

"Let's just say you won't be restricted to two dimensions."

"Umm…okay." Bill shifted in his seat. "But before I do anything else, I gotta take a mean piss."

"Of course, there's a toilet behind that door."

"You mean go in there?" Bill had never relieved himself in anything but an outhouse or the open countryside since he had been a child in cloth diapers.

"Yes. Just go in there and there's a seat, or you can stand if you like."

Bill unfastened his restraining belts and then stood up and stretched again. He found he was stiff all over from sleeping so long in one position and had a little trouble balancing in the moving tank. His old injuries ached as he made his way to the door and opened it. Inside was a small room with a sink on the wall and a raised seat on the floor with a large hole in it. He had seen porcelain toilets, usually among the rubble of houses, but had never actually used one. Everything in here was made of shiny metal, including the toilet. There was clear water in the bottom of the hole that sloshed gently from side to side. He closed the door and had a little trouble with the suit but managed to get it unzipped and down around his ankles. It took him a minute to get a stream going, but when he did it seemed like he would never stop.

When he finally got the suit back on, he walked out of the room. Samuel was looking at him.

"Did you wash your hands?"

"What?" Bill was puzzled.

"Okay, I can see we have a lot to teach you." Samuel got out of his chair and walked past Bill to the toilet. "You see these levers?" He turned one of the spigots and water began to pour out of the spout above the sink. "You get your hands wet, then use this soap." There was a small bar in a depression next to the sink. He demonstrated and then wiped his clean hands on a hanging towel.

"Why?"

"Well, there are things called germs—"

"Yeah, I remember my mother talking about them. Make you sick."

"That's right. Well I'm sure she told you to wash your hands before you eat, right?"

"Yep. But we didn't have soap very often. Some of the women in the town make it out of lye, but you're liable to take off a layer or two of skin if you use it too much. They only use it for dishes and clothes and such."

Samuel smiled. "Well, this soap is much milder and it kills those germs, so you don't get sick as often. You can even use it to bathe."

"Well, we'll see about that. It's a little too cold out for takin' a bath."

Samuel smiled again. "Not where we're going. I think you're going to enjoy this. Oh, and after using the facilities, you can get rid of waste by pressing this lever." He flushed the toilet and Bill watched the water swirling out of the bowl.

"Seems kind of wasteful, using clear water for that…wherever it went."

"Don't worry, it gets filtered and then it's even cleaner than it started out to be. I think you'll find we don't waste much. Can't afford to. We then re-use it for cooking and even drinking."

Bill grimaced at the thought of drinking used water but considered it for a moment and said, "Well, I do know a thing or two about not being wasteful."

Samuel smiled broadly, "Good! I see that once again The Traveler has chosen wisely. Now, if you'll wash up, we can tuck into that stew."

Bill washed his hands and returned to his seat. The wonderful aroma emitted from the pot made his stomach rumble. He thought again and looked at the pot. "I am hungry, but I'm just not too sure about eating filtered-pee stew."

Chapter 12

Fred Johnson and Jose Fernandez slept near a smoldering fire on the bank of the Nueces River. They were in thin sleeping bags that were threadbare but managed to keep most of the cold air out. Their saddles made for somewhat uncomfortable pillows. The horses were tied to a mesquite tree slightly higher on the bank and were becoming restless. Something was in the river, moving silently upstream toward the sleeping men—something huge.

The horses began to whinny loudly and prance about, pulling on their reins. Both men woke simultaneously and grabbed their rifles. Small waves began lapping onto the previously still shore, and the men turned toward the river. After shucking the sleeping bags, they rose to their feet. Jose grabbed a handful of twigs and threw them on the coals. In a few seconds they flared to life, casting some light on their surroundings. In the meager illumination, they could see two reflected lights in the water a few yards from the shore. The lights were about fourteen inches apart and stopped their advance when the fire brightened. Nictitating lenses briefly dulled the eyes of the enormous alligator as it regarded the men hungrily. The horses were becoming frantic.

Suddenly the water exploded as the thirty-five foot reptile charged. The men backed away as quickly as they could, and before the fire was put out by the dripping beast, they could see it had too many legs—four on one side and three on the other, some of them dragging uselessly. It made straight for Fred, and if he hadn't tripped over a hidden log in the grass, it probably would have gotten him. He heard the dripping jaws snap shut over his prone body as he lay motionless in the grass, frozen with fear. The foul-smelling creature stopped and moved its head slowly back and forth over Fred, wondering what had happened to its prey. It began to back toward the water. Fred watched with huge eyes as it moved away from him in the star light. He realized he hadn't been breathing and began whooping air in and out loudly. The alligator stopped and listened to the noise. Fred clapped a hand over his own mouth and sat still. The creature listened a few moments longer and then moved back toward the water, finally disappearing beneath the black surface. It had been strangely uninterested in, or perhaps even bothered by, the horses. Its stench remained heavy in the air.

After a short while, Jose called out quietly in a thick Spanish accent, "Fret! You alive?"

Fred was still staring at where the alligator had vanished silently into the water and didn't answer at first.

"Fret!"

"Yeah, yeah, I'm okay," Fred said breathlessly and began to search for his rifle. He didn't remember dropping it, but it wasn't with him anymore. He found it near the ruined fire where he had let go of it as soon as the alligator had charged. It was covered in mud and would have to be cleaned.

Jose was trying to calm the horses, and Fred moved quickly to help him. "Let's get away from the water. We'll come back for our gear when it's daylight."

"Son a bitch! Did you see that thing? I almost chitted my pants."

"Yeah, yeah," he repeated, "you see one giant deformed alligator, you've seen 'em all." He was trying to sound nonchalant, but truth be told he felt the need to check his own pants. "Let's get higher up the bank and build another fire."

"Okay. Madre de Dios. You must have iron huevos. I thought it got you."

They had been traveling northeast all the previous day and had yet to find the trail. The town mentioned by The Boss was miles south of them, and their low profile had kept them undetected. Once darkness had approached, Fred decided to stop for the night by the river. They had fished for a while using some salted pork for bait but hadn't caught anything. Fred thought he knew why, now. They had to resort to their packed food supply for supper, knowing they had to live off the land as much as possible in order to make it last. But obviously they had traveled north far enough to encounter deformed wildlife, so they had to be careful what they ate. Maybe the river had brought the radiation from farther north and it had affected the gator. Regardless, they would have to check any game they found and be mindful of any deformities before they ate it.

They decided on a spot under a large cottonwood and built another fire with some sticks they found scattered under the tree, sitting and talking until dawn.

The horses, now calmed from their previous ordeal, were once again securely tied nearby.

When it was light enough to see, they returned to their destroyed campsite. The alligator had run through the camp on its working legs but had returned to the water by scuffling sideways as it turned, destroying some of the equipment. One of the radios was crushed into the mud and was now so many pieces of useless metal, plastic, glass, and wire. The saddles were mostly unharmed, though the contents of the saddlebags were scattered in the grass—including the packed food. Fortunately, it was too cold for insects to be at it. Jose brushed the dried grass and dirt from it as much as he could and re-packed it.

Fred found the remaining radio pack and switched it on. "Base, this is Scout One. Do you read?" Moments of static hiss passed. He repeated the call and listened.

Finally a sleepy female voice replied, "Scout One, this is base, read you loud and clear." The last part was spoken through a yawn.

Fred replied with some sarcasm, "So sorry to wake you from your comfortable nap, but we need to give a progress report."

"Go ahead, Scout One," she said, more awake this time.

"We suffered an animal attack, one radio destroyed, food supply..." he looked at Jose, who shrugged his shoulders and gave a quick thumbs-up, "...slightly soiled, but okay. Other equipment also soiled, but okay. Have not encountered vehicle tracks as yet. Continuing search."

"Copy, Scout One. Will relay."

"Scout One, out."

He switched off the radio and looked at Jose, who was saddling his horse. "Damn dispatch, anyway. Now there's an easy job."

"Yeah, that was Shirley." He pronounced it *Chirley*. "I heard she takes it real nice. Don't complain so much. Too fat for me, though."

"Oh, like you can afford to be picky."

"Hey, you chut up your mouth. I do okay."

Fred laughed. "Yeah, right. One time, and she was shit-faced."

"I don't care. Drunk, sober, it all feels the same."

"I have to admit, she did feel good, even if it was sloppy seconds."

"You mean...you?!"

"Yeah, after you left. And I wasn't the last one, either."

Jose laughed out loud. "Son a bitch. You one sick bastardo!"

"Yeah, I get by." Fred was putting a saddle on his own horse and then shouldered the radio pack, its long whip antenna swaying as he gathered other equipment.

After the camp was packed up, they mounted the horses and chewed on deer jerky as they started downriver in search of a place to cross. The jerky had a little sand on it, and they had to spit periodically. The sun was now peeking over the horizon, and soon they found a shallow section of fast-moving water. They crossed without incident, looking around diligently for any sign of the monster from the night before.

"I say we go due east now, try to stay south of dead zones," Fred said, referring to irradiated areas of the land. The brush here was thick, and deer trails had to be followed in order to make their way through. Sometimes it was too thick and they had to dismount. "If they were in tanks, they must have used an old road."

"The Boss, he say they go northeast from the town. We chould run into a road going that way sometime today. I saw one on the map."

"Yeah, if we don't run into something like that 'gator first. Or something even uglier."

Jose crossed himself and said quietly, "Aye Dios mio."

Chapter 13

Samuel was flipping switches and turning knobs while looking at one of the view screens. "We'll be arriving soon. We're about three miles from the base."

Bill had been sitting and staring at a different view screen, quietly watching old buildings pass by, now illuminated by morning light. Some were quite large and filled with many broken windows. He was thinking about what it must have been like in the pre-war days. Abandoned cars and trucks had been pushed off the road and stood like silent sentinels, guarding the abundance of the past from ever returning. What now made him hopeful of mankind surviving was the discovery of these new-found and obviously advanced people. In their technology, and more subtly in their attitude, they seemed to be ignoring the imminent doom of all humans. He had been struggling to survive for as long as he could remember, always wondering from where, or even *if* his next meal would come. These people seemed to take plentiful food and shelter for granted, and that freed up the ability to concentrate on other projects—like building these tanks.

He thought about the massacre the day before. Turning toward Samuel, he said, "I gotta say, you guys are certainly impressing me with all this stuff. How did you come up with it?"

"What do you mean?" Samuel was still looking at the screen and adjusting the equipment.

"Well, like these tanks. If I hadn't seen it with my own eyes, I wouldn't have believed that slaughter yesterday. Them blue lights cuttin' those bastards in half. I mean, it seems like something out of a storybook. And bullets just bouncing' off this thing, even that ball on top. I never seen anything like it." Bill was smiling darkly at the memories.

Samuel turned toward Bill. He was a little put-off by the smile. "Mr. Stratton, we take the death of even one bandit very seriously. Yesterday's *demonstration* was very necessary to convince you and your friends that we are serious and that they would be safe in allowing you to come with us. Even though the bandits would have probably killed everyone in your town, it is very unfortunate so many of them had to die at our hands. However, if the mission is successful, it will all have been worth it."

Bill sat forward in his chair. "You gave them better than they deserved, if you ask me. And there you go with that mission crap again. I swear, if you don't tell me what that's all about, I'm gonna have to—"

"All in due time, Mr. Stratton. As I have said before, you will be briefed completely, and then it will become clear. For the time being, it is of the utmost importance that you remain patient." Samuel paused and softened a little. "You are a very important part of this mission, and I wish I could explain it all to you, but I have my orders."

Bill sat back and thought for a while. He turned toward the screen again and saw that they were going under an old overpass that had partially collapsed. The world was crumbling, yet these people seemed to be trying to fix it.

Looking around at the interior of the tank, he said, "All right, I'll try and be patient. You guys *are* impressive, like I said before."

"Well, you haven't seen anything yet. Wait until we get to our base and see what we have going on there. Then you can be impressed. Here, take a look. Tell me what you see." He turned the screen toward Bill on a swivel. In the distance ahead, Bill saw the road, which was almost completely paved here, continue toward the base of a hill. The domed hill, which was about three hundred feet high and who knew how wide, was covered in brown grass and had copses of leafless trees here and there. A footpath could be seen meandering up one side.

"What am I supposed to be looking at?"

"Well, tell me what you see," Samuel repeated.

"I see the road ending at the base of a hill. Oh, and I see another one of these tanks near where the road ends."

"Is that all you see?"

"Umm, yeah, pretty much."

"Excellent. What you're actually looking at is our base. And it's your new home…for a while, anyway."

"I'm supposed to be living on a hill?"

"Just wait, you'll see." Samuel turned a knob and Bill realized they had been looking at a magnified view. The hill shrank away into the distance on the screen and he could see that they were still a couple of miles from it. "I told you it was a good place to hide here."

They traveled in silence for a while and Bill returned to watching the countryside roll by. He noticed some lush gardens and saw people working in them, wondering how they got crops to grow in the winter or in irradiated land this close to an attack. He thought about asking but supposed that any answers given would only raise more questions. There were also fenced-in areas with food animals in them. Deer and some other animals he didn't recognize were behind some very tall fences, with cattle, goats, and pigs behind shorter ones. Once again the questions were building up and trying to break through the wall of his willpower.

It was almost more than he could handle when Samuel finally said, "We're here."

Bill watched the screen in front of Samuel as the tank rolled to a stop. Nothing but the road disappearing into the base of the hill could be seen. Suddenly a section of the hill in front of the tank split apart to a height of about twelve feet. Bill could see that it was an enormous set of double doors, covered in grass and about a foot-and-a-half thick, and they were swinging out to reveal a cavernous interior. The tank started forward again and made a sharp left once inside. Bill couldn't believe what he was seeing as his eyes moved from screen to screen. The entire hill was hollow! The tank drove about one hundred yards along one wall and then stopped. Samuel hit the button next to the door of the tank, and it opened.

Samuel stepped outside and beckoned for Bill to follow. Curtis, who had remained silent for most of the trip, stayed at his station flicking switches, apparently shutting down the tank. Bill released the straps and stood up, barely noticing his stiffness this time. He was riveted by the scene outside. He slowly descended the steps to a concrete floor and looked up. The underside of the hill was so high and distant in the center of the huge room that it was difficult to see. There seemed to be a mist that obscured any details, but at various locations very bright lights were suspended from it. There were buildings inside, some of them almost as tall as the sky-scrapers he had seen on his way here. A veritable small city of structures stretched before him. They were all painted white. In fact, almost everything in here was painted white, except the interior walls of the hill, which were very dark. He turned to see that the convoy of tanks had followed them inside and was now parked and unloading crew members. Already used to this spectacle, the returned personnel were busying themselves with various tasks. Several of them glanced at Bill and smiled at his clearly stunned expression. A soft "boom" signaled the closing of the double doors where they had entered.

Samuel was standing next to Bill and watching him take it all in. "Now, Mr. Stratton," he said, "you can be impressed."

Chapter 14

Fred stopped his horse with a pull on the reins and a soft, "Whoa." He was looking at the tracks left by the convoy only hours earlier. The scouts were correct in assuming the tanks would follow the old road northeast.

Jose said, "Chit, would you look at that. They dint even try to hide their tracks." The pavement here was exposed in places, but cracked and weed-covered. Most of it was dust, and there were two ruts down the middle, as if several vehicles had passed this way.

"Yeah, almost like they want us to follow. Keep your eyes peeled for an ambush."

Jose once again crossed himself. "Looks like they came and went the same way." Some of the weeds were bent or broken toward one direction, some the other.

Fred reached behind himself and switched on the radio. He keyed the mike and said, "Base, this is Scout One."

"Go ahead Scout One." The reply was muffled by some static.

"Base, we have encountered tracks heading northeast on road—stand by." He pulled out a mini map from a shirt pocket and studied it for a couple of seconds. "Looks like on road fifty-nine."

"Copy that Scout One. Road fifty-nine, following tanks northeast."

"Scout One out." He stowed the map and switched off the radio.

"Let's stay alert." Fred said and kicked his horse gently to get it started up the road.

* * *

The old mutant mountain lion had been following the two men on horses for some time now. She stopped and crouched when they stopped, and crept through the brush softly when they moved again, always staying down-wind. She was huge, standing about five feet at the shoulder, and had a large knot at the end of her hairless stubby tail, which hung useless and bumped softly against her hind legs when she walked. She still managed to remain almost silent as she followed her prey. In addition to her large size, she had one other deformity—her teeth. The normally large canines of the puma were extra long and sharp. Perhaps this was due to ordinarily recessive genes from one of her ancestors becoming activated by the radioactivity from the area to the north, where her mother had roamed while she carried her unborn litter. Regardless of the source of the teeth, they had helped the creature become an efficient killer.

She had stopped and listened patiently when the men had come across the tracks left by the stinking vehicles that had come this way earlier. She could smell the tantalizing odors they produced, these men on horses, and her nose quivered. They had made their human noises and then began following the tracks. This was good. There was a place ahead the mountain lion knew well—a place where she had killed many times before. The deer, cattle, and buffalo had often followed this trail as it dipped into a place that was cut through a small hill. The mutant cougar would wait on one side of the hill and jump down on her unsuspecting prey before they even knew she was there.

In anticipation of feeling her claws and teeth sinking into the soft victims, she quickened her pace but was careful to remain undetected.

* * *

Jose said, "What you think The Boss is gonna give us if we lead him to these bastardos?"

"I don't know, but it's gonna be good. You can bet on that." Fred was looking around, searching for details of the landscape. It was the little things that were missed that got you killed. Up ahead, the road began a descent through a cut in a small hill and into a shallow valley beyond. He stopped his horse again.

Jose stopped next to him. "You see it too, huh," he said quietly. Immediately beyond the hill, a set of wheel tracks turned away from the road into the soft sand of the shoulder on the right, and disappeared into the brush. "Looks like a good place for an ambush."

Fred nodded and pulled his reins to the left, turning his horse to find a route around this place. Jose sat for a moment looking at the tracks, then shook his head at the stupidity of the ones they pursued. He turned his horse quietly to follow Fred back the way they had come.

* * *

The cougar was almost to the top of the hill when she stopped. Something wasn't right. She felt that she wasn't alone in waiting for the prey. She raised her head and sniffed the air. From her right came the stinking smell of those vehicles, very strong now. She looked that way and saw a shiny ball on a post, sticking up from just past the hill. The sight was so strange, she started and then crouched. A low growl issued from her throat as she stared at it. She could sense that it was dangerous—deadly, even. It was too much for her and she retreated, vanishing into the brush. She would have to look elsewhere for her meal.

* * *

Jason Bider sat patiently inside the tank, drinking herbal tea and reading an old novel. The weapons were deployed and the alarms were set. If anything bigger than a rabbit came into range, the computer would notify him. Unfortunately it could not see through solid rock, and nothing would be detected until it emerged from the small canyon cut into the hill. Already some deer had come down the trail, as had a pack of peccary.

Once again, the computer spoke up, "Intruder detected." Jason put down the book and looked at the weapons screen. A large red blob was approaching from the south. He looked at the view screen connected to the camera in the laser ball. Something big and tan-colored was moving through the brush, very nimbly. He adjusted the screen and zoomed in on the target. The face of a huge and angry looking mountain lion leapt into view. He adjusted another knob, which picked up minute sounds, and heard the low rumble of a growl. That, and the sight of the large upper canines protruding a full four inches below the lower jaw made Jason's skin crawl, even though he knew he was protected inside the armored tank.

His finger hovered over the fire button, but the large cat quickly turned and retreated silently from sight. He watched its red blob until it disappeared from the targeting screen. Calming himself, he took another sip of tea, made a final check of the sensors, and returned to reading his book.

Chapter 15

Craig sat at his desk and stared at the progress report in front of him. Comms office had been in touch with the scouts and they had found the trail. Soon they would find the location of the "civilized" enemy, and then The Boss and his followers could take what was rightfully theirs. He had listened to their leader describe the toys they had now—tanks with laser weapons. How did they get this technology, anyway? And what the hell was a laser? No matter. Their own tanks would be ready soon, if that damn incompetent Smith would pull his head out of his ass, that is. He decided to make an immediate, personal visit to the refurbishing facility and got up from his desk. Passing by the comms office, he told the operator where he was going in case The Boss needed him and walked out to his car.

As Craig drove the old beat up Chevy through the streets of what was once Laredo, he was thinking of a strategy for fighting the laser tanks. He didn't know if the lasers could penetrate the hulls of the Army tanks, but he didn't think they could. At any rate, he would make sure their own gunners targeted any tank attacking them as quickly as possible and then blow it to hell. Unfortunately, their ammunition was limited, so practice for the gunners was restricted to five shots at a medium-range target and a few hundred rounds with the machine guns. At the top of the hill overlooking the facility, Craig stopped. The sight of the nearly forty tanks lined up under their overhangs was impressive. The tanks still being refurbished had attending crews, and small cranes were moving around some of them. They were mostly M-48 "Patton" tanks and weighed in at over forty-five tons each. The turrets with their 90mm guns were especially dangerous-looking, and he smiled at the thought of the flimsy enemy tanks exploding under their fire.

He continued down the hill and parked near the closest tank. As Craig got out, he heard raised voices coming from the shed that served as the engineer's office. Smith was apparently meeting some opposition from his chief foreman. He quietly approached the door and listened.

"I don't want to hear it! The Boss said two weeks, and if that means working double shifts, then that's what they'll do!"

Dick Lawson, the foreman, sounded tired. "But I'm telling you they're exhausted already! We lost two good mechanics yesterday because an overworked crane operator crushed them by accident. We can't afford to lose any more men."

"Okay, I'll just go to The Boss and tell him the men are a little tired, so he'll just have to wait two additional weeks for his tanks. Then you can be the Chief around here because I'll be dead, and then *you* can tell him why he has to wait. Sound good?"

At the mention of The Boss, Lawson had stiffened. He looked at Smith for a moment and sighed wearily. "No. I see your point. Double shifts it is."

Craig appeared in the door and asked, "Is there a problem?"

Smith jumped slightly and said, "No! Not anymore."

"Then The Boss can count on his tanks in two weeks?"

"Absolutely. If I have to finish them myself."

"Good," he looked at the two men, "because I wouldn't want to have to tell him otherwise. And Smith, you pull this off and there will be a nice reward in it for you. Maybe you can have one of my leftover women or something." He turned to walk back to his car and called over his shoulder, "'Bout time you grew a pair."

Chapter 16

Bill sat in his new home and ate hungrily. The food here was incredible. Chicken with rice, greens with bacon, and some herbal tea sweetened with actual sugar. He hadn't tasted sugar in many years, with the exception of the feast, and couldn't get over how good sweet food and drink tasted. Ellen was sitting near the door with the cart of food, watching him with a subtle smile. As he cleaned up his plate with a piece of cornbread, she asked, "Would you like some more?"

"Yes, ma'am, keep it coming. This is mighty good." He held out his plate and she refilled it with the prepared food from the pots on the tray.

"I'll send your compliments to the chefs." Ellen smiled sweetly.

"You do that." He began on his second plateful, but more slowly this time. He had been given a short tour of the underground city earlier and was amazed by their technology. There were factories, stores, housing, and recreation centers—all inside the hill. As he was shown around by the friendly staff, his distrust melted away. These people were not agents of the bandits and were in no way associated with them. They all seemed excited and happy to see him— that much was clear. He felt no threat from any of them. They were an advanced, productive society that seemed focused and very civilized. Once again he allowed himself to feel a little hope.

After his tour, he was escorted to his quarters by Ellen. She had shown him his bed with white sheets, blankets, and two goose-down pillows. Everything in the room, including the walls, floor, and ceiling, was white, and although there seemed to be no light source, the room was completely illuminated in a pleasant way. A bathroom, also in white, was inside a door next to his bed, and she had shown him how to work the sink, toilet, and shower—a real shower. His mother had told him how she used to love the shower, especially when it was scalding hot on an icy cold day. After Ellen left him to go retrieve his lunch, he had taken a shower for the first time in his life, and he saw what his mother was talking about.

He smiled at Ellen. "And I have to tell you, that shower felt powerful good."

"I'm glad you liked it. You look better. I have to leave you now because you're expecting a very important visitor, and he would like to meet with you alone. I'll be back later for the dishes." With that she walked out of the room. The door automatically opened and closed as she did so.

Bill continued to eat in silence, periodically looking at the door or around the room. He wasn't sure about all this, but the food and the showers he could get used to.

"Hello, William." The voice seemed to come from inside his head. He jumped a little and then froze. "Please don't be alarmed. I know this is a new sensation for you, but you will soon get used to it." It was not unpleasant, but a little disconcerting. It was the voice of a small man, but it sounded authoritative—and yet somehow kind. He looked around the room, not quite sure what to think. "I'm speaking to you telepathically. If you wish to say something, go ahead. I'll hear you."

"What...who?" Bill said aloud.

"My name is Russell. I am the leader of this community, and I am the one who sent for you. I am the one the people here call The Traveler. We have a very important mission that involves you."

"Yeah, so I've heard. Where are you?" he said, looking around.

"I'm in a room down the hall from yours. I apologize for not coming in personally to meet with you, but I felt you needed to be prepared before that happens. You see, I will look a little strange to you, and I wish to explain that first."

"Okay, explain."

"Direct and to the point—that's one of the things I like about you, William. All right, from the beginning. I was born not too far from here, eight months after the war. I was one of a set of twins. Both my brother and I were exposed to radiation while in the womb, and it caused us to be deformed, although in very different ways. It seems one of the side effects of radiation is gene alteration. I don't expect you to know what that means, but let's just say it means our bodies started to grow in a different direction from that which is considered to be…normal. In my brother's body, recessive genes were awakened, and he grew to be what was called, in some history books, a Neanderthal. This was a different species than modern men, but there was probably some cross-breeding a long time ago. He is now something you may have heard called a caveman."

At that moment a picture formed in his mind of a tall, muscular man with much hair on his face and body, and a stooped posture. His brow jutted over his eyes, and he looked very primitive and somewhat animalistic. Bill did not know where the picture came from, but it was very clear—and a little familiar.

"There, do you see?" Russell asked.

"Yes…did you make me see that?"

"I simply sent you a mental image. In time everyone will learn to communicate this way because it saves so much time. That is, they will if we are successful in our mission. Now, to continue. In my body, the effect was the exact opposite, and I grew into what Man will eventually become…in a couple of million years. Both of us have advanced abilities, such as this telepathy. There are other abilities, such as this."

Suddenly the teapot from the tray rose into the air a few inches, floated toward Bill, and refilled the cup on the small table in front of him. Bill's eyes widened as he was overcome with fear, which froze him in his chair.

Russell continued, "I don't mean to startle you." The teapot floated back to the tray and settled with a small clink. "I just wanted to show you some of the things we are capable of, my brother and I."

Bill was breathing rapidly and managed to calm himself down. "All right, I'm impressed."

Russell laughed pleasantly, "Rest assured, William, I mean you no ill intent. We are in need of your services and mean to keep you safe. My brother, on the other hand, would like nothing more than to see you dead, as well as myself and all the people in this community. It has been very difficult to hide from him, but so far we have been able to. I'm afraid that in retrieving you, we may have tipped our hand."

"What do you mean?"

"Well, he has sent scouts to follow the convoy back here. So far they have eluded our attempts to stop them. I need them captured alive. But if they locate our hidden community and get a message back to my brother, I'm afraid he will attack."

"Wait a minute. Your brother is—"

"The leader of the bandits, yes."

Bill took a moment to think. "But that means you—"

"Rest assured, I am not in league with him. Even though he is my family, he is considered a bitter enemy."

"Good. I wouldn't mind seeing every bandit dead."

"Yes, that's one of the things we have to work on. But for now, I would like to meet you in person, if I may."

"Sure. After seeing that floating teapot trick, I think I'm ready for anything."

"Very well."

After a few moments the door opened. A short man-like creature with gray skin and a disproportionally large head stepped in. Its large black eyes were almond shaped and sloped upward at the corners. There were no external ears or nose, only vertical slits on the sides of its head and between the eyes. Its small mouth was a thin line below the nose slits. It was wearing a tailor-made white jumpsuit that didn't hide its thin limbs, and it had hands with very long fingers. It patiently allowed Bill to stare at it for a while before walking forward slowly with its right hand extended.

"Hello again, William," said Russell's voice in his head. The small mouth didn't emit the words, but it did smile slightly at Bill's shocked expression.

Slowly Bill found the self-control to extend his own hand, and he shook Russell's proffered one. The grip was surprisingly strong for such a small thin creature. "You're…."

"Yes," the voice in his head continued, "I'm Russell. As I told you, preparation for my appearance was necessary. But like many other new things soon to come, you will get used to it."

Chapter 17

Jose asked Fred, "What can you see?"

They were lying in a small depression on a hill behind which the horses were hidden. They had picked up the trail again after traveling around the ambush area in a wide circle. After a while of moving in silence, Jose had spotted a column of smoke on the horizon to the left of the road, and they had decided to investigate.

Fred was looking through an old pair of binoculars. "Looks like a farm. Single house, pen with a few pigs, chickens in the yard, and a garden. Easy pickin's. We won't go hungry tonight."

"Good. I'm tired of eating that dried meat chit."

At that moment a young, slender woman in old blue jeans and a flannel shirt emerged from the front door and walked toward the chicken hut. She was carrying a basket, probably to gather eggs. "Wait a minute…what have we here?" Fred watched as her shoulder-length blond hair trailed behind her in the breeze.

Jose was also looking down at the farm, but without visual aid. "Is that what I think it is?"

"It's exactly what you think it is. We won't be lonely tonight either."

"Mamasita! Just make sure we take care of any, uh, distractions first."

"That's right. We'll wait here and watch until just before dark, which I calculate is about…" he looked at the setting Sun, "one more hour. Then we'll flank the house and try to look in through those windows before we go in. Way I see it, we gotta eat and sleep tonight. Might as well do it in a cabin with a nice hostess, willin' or not." He handed the binoculars to Jose. "You watch while I take a nap." At that he rolled onto his back and found he was quite comfortable in the shallow depression.

Jose looked at him with a little contempt. "Pinche gringo," he muttered. Fred just smiled without opening his eyes. Then Jose looked at the farm through the binoculars, but the girl still hadn't emerged from the hut yet. When she finally did, he eyed her hungrily. From what he could tell, she had a pretty face and an ample bosom above her slim waist. This was going to be a good night.

* * *

Ramey's body sat cross-legged on the floor of his private room with a single candle in front of it. The shelves had been restocked with the best China that could be found, though the pickings had been slim lately. The body's eyes were closed and it seemed to have become a vacated shell, which it was.

Ramey moved over the landscape following the trail the scouts were on. He saw the ambush tank on the other side of the little hill. He also saw the tracks of his scouts and how they had diverted around the ambush. They were good. He followed them quickly to the hill, where they watched the farm. Their conversation had drifted up to him. Well, wasn't this nice. They were going to have a little fun along the way, when they should be closing in on his brother. He thought of coming back to his body and calling them on the radio. He detested using telepathy because he was clumsy at it, usually scrambling the minds of the receptors beyond repair. Instead, he decided to try to find his brother again.

He continued northeast at great speed, hoping to penetrate the wall he had always hit. After a few seconds of blurring travel, it happened again. *Wham!* The harder he hit, the more stunned he became, and he was disoriented for more than three minutes this time, wandering aimlessly around the area. Sometimes he bumped lightly into the wall, finding it somehow amusing. When he came to his senses, he explored the wall as he had countless times before. He moved left and right several hundred miles and even tried to rise above it as high as into space, but it seemed endless. It stank of his brother, *the bastard*. His scouts were the only way in for now.

He soon tired of this game and returned to the scouts. They were no longer on the hill, but were now flanking the house in the growing darkness. He decided to stay a while and watch. Maybe watching a nice rape would lighten his mood. Yeah. He would worry about his brother later.

As he watched his scouts approach the house, he noticed movement from the north. The farmer was returning from hunting on horseback. He was still about a half mile from home, and he had a small, dead deer across his lap. Ramey decided to practice his telepathy with the farmer. As delicately as he could, he grasped the farmer's mind and began to control it. There. A lovely huge dragon appeared in the path about a hundred feet ahead of the farmer. The man on horseback stopped and stared at the creature only he could see in the fading light. It was green with huge wings, yellow horns and angry red eyes, which turned to him. It stared at him for a moment and then sucked in audibly and blew out a great gout of fire in his direction. The farmer screamed and scrambled to turn his horse around. The flames hit his back, and only he saw that they ignited the brush around him as he kicked his horse, trying to make it run. He felt himself burning and screamed again, this time in agony. There were no real flames, but blisters did appear on the man's back. The bewildered horse finally started to run, and the deer dropped off, un-noticed by the farmer. Suddenly, the man's face went slack as the horse continued running, and a few moments later he dropped off, with one foot still in the stirrup. The horse dragged him for miles, but he never noticed. His mind was gone. Eventually his body died as it was dragged through the brush over rocks and logs.

Ramey had watched all this with great interest and then cursed to himself as he felt the farmer's mind turn to mush in his grasp. *Oh well, no big loss.* Time to go back and watch his scouts with the farmer's wife. That should prove to be entertaining, at the very least.

Chapter 18

The following morning, Bill was preparing for his training to begin. Shortly after his visit from Russell the afternoon before, he had been taken to a recreation area where he sat and watched some of the young people from the community playing what they called "basketball." When he was approached by the youngsters and asked to join a game, he politely declined saying he just wanted to watch. He had never seen team sports and was fascinated by the concept, even though he didn't know the rules.

He had then returned to his room and gotten into bed, sleeping soundly until morning. It was the first actual bed he had been in for as long as he could remember. He thought it was too soft for him to sleep in at first, but before he knew it, he was out. Upon awakening, his breakfast of scrambled eggs and fresh cold milk was brought in by Ellen, who told him he would begin his training after he ate. He asked if there was time for another shower, and she smiled and told him yes, but only a quick one.

After a scalding shower, he dressed in a fresh jumpsuit and sat patiently, thinking about everything that had happened to him since his arrival. He was startled again by the voice in his head. "Hello, William. I trust you slept well?"

"Oh…yes. Very well."

"Good." The door opened and Russell walked in. "I see you're enjoying our accommodations," he said, walking past the mostly empty food cart.

"Yes I am. But I'm kind of feelin' like I need to do some work to earn my keep."

Russell smiled, "That's one of the qualities that makes you right for this mission. If you are ready, we can begin the training immediately."

"Sounds good to me."

"Very well. First of all, a little more about my abilities. In addition to telepathy and telekinesis, which you've already seen, you should know I have the ability to travel to distant places without my body and to see and hear what is happening there. That is how we acquired the technology to build the tanks, to keep the hill which is hiding this city from collapsing, and to make the power plants to run everything. You see, this technology already exists elsewhere, but not on this planet."

"Not on this planet? You mean—"

"Yes. When I say travel to distant places, I mean to other civilizations in the universe. Some of them are very friendly and advanced, and they can communicate with me when I visit them. Earth itself is very primitive, it even was before the war. I have been able to bring this technology back with me and convey it to the builders here, like this."

Bill saw a series of images flash through his mind. There were blueprints, factory workers working on electronics, machines that were moving and building other machines, and finally the tanks firing their weapons at targets.

"Wow." It was all he could manage.

"It has taken decades to accomplish all this, but we have a common goal in mind. That goal is to save mankind from dying. And you, William, are a very important part of accomplishing that goal."

Bill was again a little astonished. "Me? Well, I don't know what I can do."

"We'll talk about that later. Right now, I still need to explain a little more about my abilities. When I travel without my physical form, my actions are limited. I can observe things but can't interact with them physically except in present time. You see, I can also travel to the past and observe events as they happened, but I can't change them. The universe we live in is fickle that way. Do you understand?"

"I guess so. You can remember stuff but can't change it?"

"No. I can actually travel there and watch events as they happened. Any place, any time. But I can't change the events, because that would take a physical presence."

"Okay. I guess I'm not getting the traveling without your body idea."

"Very well. The physical universe we live in consists of four elements."

"Wait! I know this because I read it in a book one time. Fire, water, earth, and air, right?"

Russell chuckled pleasantly. "Not exactly. That is a concept that has become antiquated over time. The actual elements are energy, space, matter, and time. They exist separately but interact with each other. They can also be used to manipulate each other. When you look around this room, you see light energy reflecting off the objects, which are matter, as they exist in their own space, and through time."

Bill looked around and considered this for a moment. "What about you? I mean when you travel without your body, what element are you?"

"That is a very good question, William. You see, you and I, and everyone else for that matter, are beings that exist apart from these elements. We occupy these physical bodies in order to manipulate our physical surroundings. Unfortunately, we have become so dependent on them that we have forgotten our other abilities...at least most of us have. But that is how I am able to be here in this room with you sometimes and you can't see me."

Bill looked at Russell, "You're here...when you're not here?"

Russell chuckled again. "Oh yes, once or twice, but not to spy on you. Just to see what you were doing so I didn't interrupt. It's how I've been observing you for some time. But since I am not part of the physical universe when I travel, you couldn't detect me with your eyes or in any other physical way. Since I am here in the present, I can manipulate things to a certain extent, even without using my body."

Suddenly Bill's now-empty plate rose from his table and floated back to his cart, settling there quietly. Russell's eyes never left Bill.

"I wish you wouldn't do that," Bill said nervously.

"Your reaction to seeing these things is normal. You have been taught over the years that they are impossible, so your sense of what you believe is real has been forced to change. This is always unsettling, but there is more. My brother and I are not the only ones who can do these things. You and everyone else on this dying world can do them, too."

"Are you going to teach me how? Is that my training?"

"I really wish we had the time for that William, but unfortunately we don't. Someday in the distant future, as I said before, all people will regain these abilities. But only if we are successful in our mission. If we fail, none of this will matter. Mankind will cease to exist."

Bill thought this over. "I've had that feeling for a long time now, with the bandits and all. Is it the same everywhere?"

"No. In some places it's worse, in some a little better. The main problem is that the planet was poisoned during the war. The high concentrations of radiation are slowly spreading and will continue to do so for the next ten thousand years. Eventually only certain small animals and insects will be left, many of them mutated to adapt to the harsh environment."

"My God."

"Time, William, is the one element we don't have enough of. Especially you."

"Me."

"Yes." Russell had been standing this whole time, but now he pulled out a chair from the table and sat opposite of Bill. "I'm afraid I have some bad news for you. At some point, you ingested something that was irradiated. When your body digested it, you contracted a rare form of cancer. It has infected your bones and is, unfortunately, incurable."

Bill was stunned. "No." He shook his head in denial.

Russell touched his hand for a moment. "I'm so sorry," he said.

Bill hung his head. This was how he had seen many of his acquaintances go over the years, with cancer eating some of them up very quickly—always painfully. It was how his own mother had died. "How much time do I have?"

"Well, that depends, William. If we complete the mission as planned, you will probably live thirty more years. If not, you may only live for one or two. But the pain will become unbearable long before it takes your body."

"But I feel fine. How do you know I have it?"

"I can sense it—it's one of my abilities. Unfortunately I can't cure it. There are many things I cannot do, and that is one of them. I have tried in several cases, but each time instead of removing the cancer, I made things worse by causing it to spread. I will not attempt it with you. Yours is in the early stages, and you won't even feel any symptoms for about a week. There are vitamins and supplements we can give you to delay its effects, though, and we will begin those tomorrow. But for now I need you to focus on your training. If we succeed, you will never have contracted the disease."

"I don't get it."

Russell thought for a moment. "Tell me, have you ever heard the saying, 'a stitch in time saves nine?'"

"It was one of my mother's favorites."

"Do you know what it means?"

"Kinda like when a rip starts in your clothes. If you make a stitch in the rip, it saves you from making nine stitches later after the rip has grown, right?"

"Precisely. Well, William, we need you to make that first stitch."

Bill became more confused. "But how? I can't even do this traveling thing you talked about. And besides, if you can't change things in the past, how do you expect me to?"

Russell looked at him for a moment, then said, "With a physical presence."

Bill stared at him silently. Suddenly a realization came over him. When he spoke it was with a voice hushed by fear and awe. "You're sending me to the past somehow."

"Yes, William. But it won't be easy. There is only one way to do it, and it is fraught with danger. Are you up for it?"

Bill thought for a moment about the things that had been revealed to him this morning. This strange little man had put a lot on him in a very short time. He thought about the plate floating magically from his table to his tray. He thought about the man before him who could communicate without talking, who could send pictures to his mind, and who probably possessed the means of sending him back in time. But weighing over all this was the news that he was dying, and that it would be a slow, painful death like so many others around him had suffered. Finally he spoke.

"The way I see it, Russell, I don't have much of a choice."

Chapter 19

The scouts were following the trail once again in the cold morning. They had killed the girl once they had finished with her the night before, after flipping an old coin to see who would go first while the other took a lookout position a short distance from the house. She had screamed her warnings of her husband's imminent return, but the man never showed. Later they had thrown her body in the brush for the scavengers. The pig and some chickens had made a welcome meal, and they had packed some supplies from the house onto their horses.

Now they were following the tracks in the road, always watchful for another ambush location. Fred reached behind himself and turned on the radio.

"Base, this is Scout One."

After a short hesitation, the reply came. "This is Base. Go ahead, Scout One." It was a male voice this time.

"We are making good time, still heading northeast."

"Copy, Scout One. Stand by for a message from The Boss." A quiet static hiss filled the pause as the two men looked at each other uneasily. The Boss almost never spoke on the radio, and when he did it was never good.

"You gentlemen have a good night?" His voice was jovial, but dripped with acid.

"Uh…yes sir."

"Yeah. You better be more careful next time. That woman's husband would have probably killed you two if I hadn't intervened, and I probably won't be there next time. You little shits are being sloppy, and it damn well better stop! Am I understood?"

Fred swallowed hard and keyed the transmitter. "Yes, sir."

"Now, listen carefully. You're about to enter an area where I can't go. You'll be on your own, so I want you to report back every hour with an update. Watch for more tanks and avoid them at all costs. When you find the headquarters at a distance, do not approach it. Just report your position and get out of there. Make note of where you are now and where their HQ is from that position. Once again, am I understood?"

"Absolutely, sir."

"I hope so. And no more side trips or I'll cut your balls off and make you eat them. Base out."

"Scout One out." Fred switched off the radio.

"Holy chit. He was watching us last night." Jose was looking at the road ahead, not really seeing it. "How does he do that?"

"We'll probably never know." Fred was looking around. "We better do what he says. He could be watching us right now."

"Son a bitch, you're right. Maybe we chould mark this spot with something."

"Way ahead of you," Fred said and got off his horse to find some rocks to pile in the road. "Help me, would ya?"

Jose dismounted and they made a large "X" with the rocks, centered on the road. The blacktop was still mostly covered with sand, but the mark was clear enough to see from a good distance. When they were finished, they mounted up and pushed ahead.

After about ten minutes of riding, the horses began a nervous, side-stepping prance and were snorting loudly. Finally they stopped and refused to go any further, still dancing and trying to back up.

"Something's got them spooked," Fred said as he pulled out his rifle. He turned his horse and rode to the side of the road where he dismounted. Jose followed suit and was watching the road ahead with his pistol drawn.

They tied the horses and moved in a crouched walk along the side of the road. Suddenly Fred hit something that felt like a soft wall. Jose, following behind, ran into his back and they both fell down backwards.

"What the hell are you doing?" Jose asked.

"I ran into something."

"What?"

"I don't know," Fred said as he stood up. He put out his hand and felt for the invisible wall in front of him. When he found it, he ran his hands along it slowly. A chill went down his spine. "This is strange. It's like a wall that isn't there—but it is."

"Loco gringo." Jose stood up and walked straight into the wall, which folded the front of his hat and knocked him back on his butt. "Ching gao! You're right!" He stood and also began to feel along the wall. He tried pushing through it and found that he could. "Lookit! I can put my hand through it."

Fred tried and found he could as well. He noticed there was pressure on him where the wall was and it pressed his sleeve into his arm. The wall seemed to be about three inches thick. He continued pushing until his entire arm was in, up to his shoulder. Withdrawing his appendage from the wall seemed to have no ill effect, and he could feel the wall close up behind his extracted hand. He looked at his hand and wiggled his fingers.

"You notice there's no sound coming from that side?"

Jose listened for a moment. "Yeah, I can hear birds and stuff back behind us, but nothing that way," he nodded in the direction they were facing.

"We have to go in slow. You go first."

"Bull chit. You go first this time. You got to go first last night."

Fred pulled out the old coin. "Call it," he said and flipped it into the air.

"Tails."

"You always pick tails." He lifted his right hand from the back of his left where he had slapped the coin. It was tails.

"Son a bitch. I finally won! You go."

Fred looked from Jose to the invisible wall, and back. "Two out of three?"

"Chit no. You go."

Fred looked at the wall he couldn't see again and shrugged. "Okay, here goes nothing." He put out both hands and pushed them through. He continued forward, and as his face got nearer he could feel his breath bounce off the wall. He instinctively closed his eyes and put his face into it. He found he couldn't breathe inside the wall and hurriedly pushed his head through, gasping for air on the other side. When he was through, he noticed something he had never felt before. While his head was in the wall, there was a sense of another presence. Someone benevolent but incredibly powerful. This feeling was like someone was there that could be his friend but who would also kill him quickly if he were crossed. It was a strange mixture of feelings. He looked back at Jose with an odd expression on his face.

Jose said, "You okay?" When Fred tried to answer, Jose couldn't hear anything he was saying. "Can you hear me?" he shouted.

Fred, who also couldn't hear Jose, backed away from the wall and pointed at his ear while shaking his head. He made gestures for Jose to follow. Jose did and had the same difficulties as Fred. He too was bewildered by the bizarre feeling.

"Did you feel that?" Jose asked, and Fred nodded silently.

"We better be careful. Whatever…or whoever is causing that is going to be one tough bastard. This must be the place where the boss can't go."

Jose turned and looked back. "I don't think we're going to get the horses through that."

"No. We'll have to go back through and get as many supplies as we can carry and free the horses. And we better mark this spot as well. I'll tell Base what we found, but they probably won't believe us."

"Yeah," said Jose. "Good luck 'splaining that one."

Chapter 20

"Time is the most difficult element to manipulate," Russell said as they walked. They had been talking in Bill's room and were now walking through the streets between the buildings in the underground city. Russell had said there was something he needed for Bill to see firsthand. They had left the room and met Ellen in the hallway as she was returning for the dishes. At that moment Bill heard Russell talking to her telepathically as he told her they were going to visit the Kronos. She had said she would radio ahead to let them know. They continued down the hall. For a moment Bill felt a twinge of something he didn't understand. Was it jealousy? This did not get past Russell, who stopped to look at him for a moment.

"You feel distress toward Ellen and I."

"No. Why do you say that?"

"I can sense something in you, but it is misplaced. We'll have to work on that as well."

As they walked in the streets, they were approaching a cluster of buildings near the center of the city. Bill could look up and see the highest point on the underside of the hill. Russell continued with the training.

"We have to use the other three elements in great quantity to change time. You will have to travel in a large ship through space, using a huge amount of energy."

"Wait, couldn't you just build a machine to send me back in time? I read a book about that once."

"Yes, I've read that book as well. Unfortunately it doesn't work that way. If you were to step out of the space-time continuum for only a few moments and then step back in, the Earth would have moved out from under you and you'd be in space. Do you see?"

"Not exactly."

"The Earth is currently moving very fast through space when compared to the center of the universe, even though to you and me it seems we are very still. In order to travel through time, it has to be done through space as well."

"Okay, I'll take your word for it."

"Trust me William, this is the only way possible…for now. We owe a great deal to a race on the other side of the galaxy for giving us this technology, but it has not been easy. Many of the materials have been difficult to come by…hold on a moment." Russell closed his eyes and stood very still for a few seconds. "It would seem my brother's scouts have penetrated the wall."

Bill looked around and said, "Wall? What wall?"

Russell chuckled again, "Oh, don't worry. They're still about a hundred miles from here. I just informed the tank command and they are en route to intercept. You see, I constructed a sort of mental energy wall around our headquarters to keep my brother from finding us. When he travels without his body, and he doesn't do so very often, he can't penetrate the wall in that form. It takes a physical presence to get through it. I have had to make it so strong that it does have an effect on the physical universe as well, but it can't stop beings from passing through it if they are physically there. It just tends to slow them down a little."

"So they're getting close?"

"Yes, in fact closer than my brother's tribe has ever been. But they're on foot now. Their horses have refused to get near the wall." Russell chuckled again.

"Damn. I wish you could teach me that stuff."

"I'm afraid I have other more pressing things to teach you right now."

They emerged from an alley between two buildings into a clearing. Bill looked ahead and stopped in his tracks. In the center of the clearing was a group of people working on a large craft sitting on four legs. It was metallic and spherical, and it dominated the scene. It was about twenty feet across and had circular, foot-wide portholes in various locations. It looked like it had four legs on the top side as well, sticking up in the air, with large circular pads on the ends of these. The workers were welding in some areas and painting in others. It was shiny silver in some places but was being painted flat black. On the side facing them, the hatch was open and Bill noticed it was very similar to the hatches on the tanks, with steps leading inside. The interior was brightly lit, and he could see several instrument panels and monitor screens—also a chair.

Russell had been watching him stand there and absorb it all.

"Impressive, isn't it? We call it the Kronos, named for the Greek god who controlled time. This, William, is your ship. And it will take you back in time for us."

Suddenly Bill was overwhelmed. He staggered a little and had to bend and grab his knees. The realization that this was all real was finally hitting home. "I...I can't..."

Russell stood patiently next to him. "It's all right, William. I know this is a lot to take in in such a short time. I would like to ease you into this slowly, but we don't have that luxury. Just remember, there is nothing I'm asking you to do that you cannot do."

"But...you want me to fly that?"

"Not exactly. I want you to fly *in* that. Other than a few maintenance chores, you won't have to do much at all. It's mostly automated, and I will control the rest while I can. I think you will find the accommodations very comfortable."

Bill felt some relief but was still bewildered. "How long will I have to be in there?"

"About eight weeks."

Slowly he stood up straight again, feeling a little more in control. "What? I have to be in that thing for that long?"

"Yes, but you won't be idle. You will continue your training, and there is even some entertainment. And don't worry, there will be plenty of food, water, and air."

"Air?"

"Yes. You will be traveling through deep space, and I'm afraid air is something you will have to bring with you. We have been given a great gift in this technology, William. The people of Earth had just begun their first tiny steps into space when the war broke out. That was one of the reasons we chose this location. A few short miles from here is a complex where we salvaged many of the parts and equipment to build this ship and its controls. Mostly though, it had to be built from scratch. Isn't it beautiful? The aluminum skin is very sturdy and light. The nuclear engines are similar to the ones we use on the tanks, only much more powerful." Russell thought for a moment. "Ironic, isn't it?"

"What do you mean?"

"Well, the same type of energy that was used to destroy the world is now going to be used to save it."

Bill looked at him. "Save the world. You sure you have the right man for this?"

"Oh, yes. You'll do fine. Now to continue, those four legs on top are actually the gravitational propulsion system. They can in fact bend gravity, the force that is holding you and me to the ground right now, and turn it upside-down creating a gravity well above the ship. Fortunately, gravity exists throughout the universe, and those pads grab it and manipulate it. The ship simply becomes heavier in an upward direction relative to the Earth, and off you will go. Do you see those doors up there in the ceiling?"

Bill looked where Russell was looking. At the very crest of the hill's underside were large double doors, big enough to let the ship through. They were barely visible in the darkness because most of the suspended lights shined downward and Bill had to squint. "Yes."

"Beyond that is the sky, and then space. You see, the air around you is also being held down with gravity and is a relatively thin layer when compared to the size of the Earth. Here, let me show you."

Suddenly Bill had images pushed into his mind again. This time he could see the Earth far below him with tiny fluffy white clouds in a field of blue. It was the most beautiful thing he had ever seen. Then he was turned and looking at an angle of the Earth where the horizon met with blackness and bright stars beyond. The horizon seemed bright blue near the surface and then faded into the blackness.

"That fuzzy section you see is the air. Where it stops is where space begins…and there is no air. If you were to open the ship in space, you would die very quickly."

Bill was a little disoriented with the view, but it was stunning. Distractedly he said, "Right, got it. Don't open the door." Russell stopped sending the pictures and Bill was back on the ground. He looked around, clearly disappointed.

Russell smiled, "Soon you will be looking out those portholes and seeing these things with your own eyes."

Bill looked at the ship as if seeing it in a new light. "When do I leave?"

"Two days. They will finish construction today, and there is a celebration tomorrow, along with a test flight. You will have to sit that one out in case there is a malfunction. But rest assured, all systems have been tested and re-tested. There won't be a mishap."

"You sound pretty sure of yourself."

"Oh, I have seen the test flight already. I can visit the future as well, but it's only reliable for a short distance. It constantly changes with our present actions. Isn't that interesting?" Russell started walking. "Now, come William. I want to show you the inside of your ship."

Chapter 21

Craig was sitting at his desk in his office when The Boss walked in.

"Progress?" Ramey asked. He seemed to be in a good mood.

"Yes, Boss. I have motivated the mechanics and we will have the tanks ready a little early."

"Good. The scouts are through the wall and getting close to my brother's headquarters. Pretty soon I'll have that little pipsqueak cornered. It's a great time to be alive, Craig!" He clapped his right-hand man hard on the shoulder.

Craig smiled through the pain and said, "Yes sir."

"Right now, I'm in the mood for a little female companionship. Find me a meat girl and send her in." He turned and left Craig's office humming a tuneless song, headed for his recreation room.

Craig immediately went out the door and down the hall in the opposite direction to the communications office. He looked in to see the operator reading again.

"What the hell did I tell you about that?"

The operator jumped in his seat and quickly threw the comic book under the desk. "Uhh...Sir!"

"Look, I don't want to kill you, but I will if I have to. And believe me you would much rather I do it than the Boss." The operator's face bloomed with embarrassment and fear. He swallowed hard. "Now, get on the horn to Supply and have them send over a meat girl for the Boss. Immediately!"

"Yes, sir!" He tuned the radio and then hesitated. "Uh, does he have any preference?"

"The same as usual, small and dark-haired, but make sure she has some fight in her. He's in a good mood right now."

"Yes, sir." He keyed the mike and delivered the order.

Russell went to the door of the building to wait. The meat girls were captured during raids and held in a warehouse known as 'Supply' under guard for The Boss whenever he wanted them. They were often young girls and easy to control, but some of the more feisty ones were held in a special area with cages. None of them knew for sure why they were held there, but many suspected it wasn't for any good reason. Most didn't question their captors because they received good food and other creature comforts. All they knew was that someone would come in once in a while and take one of them somewhere else, never to return.

* * *

Jim Lankford, the head guard, took the radio order in his small corner office and walked into the warehouse. Some of the girls were in groups talking quietly, and others were eating at picnic tables. The supplies were getting a little low, he noticed.

"Dole!" he called to one of the guards who were watching the group that was eating. "New order. Special." Dole stood and followed him wordlessly. At the back there were two girls in the cages. One contained a buxom blond who stared bullets through her captors. The other held a sly-looking, petite, raven-haired girl of about twenty who was wearing a long-sleeved flannel shirt with an ankle-length skirt. Her clothes were tattered and dirty.

He walked to the second girl's cage and fished for his keys. "Well, now. What's your name, honey?"

She looked at him angrily, and then her face changed. Suddenly she became very sweet and said, "Lyla," with a coy smile on her face.

"Okay, Lyla, this is your lucky day. You're getting moved to the main house where you'll be a servant to The Boss. You will be doing some chores, but you'll also be given free time each day. Now doesn't that sound nice?"

"Oh, yes sir, Mister Guard Man. That sounds much better than being cooped up in here." The smile on her lips did not touch her eyes.

Jim turned to Dole and spoke softly. "Watch this one. She's trouble." Turning back to Lyla he said, "Now, I'm going to open the cage and you're going to follow me, with Dole here behind you, okay?"

"Whatever you say…sir."

Jim put the key in the lock and turned it, looking her in the eyes as he did so. He opened the door slowly and stepped back as she walked out. "Just to make sure there's no trouble, I'm going to put these handcuffs on you. It's just to keep things civil, and then when we get to the main house I'll take them off so you can clean up a little."

She pouted at this and said, "Aww, you don't have to worry about little ol' me making any fuss."

"It's standard procedure, ma'am." He reached behind himself and produced a pair of police handcuffs from the pouch on his belt. As he was opening them, she saw her chance. She dropped to the floor and reached under her dress in one move. Both guards tried to react but were too slow. Out came a sharpened piece of metal with a makeshift wooden handle which she quickly shoved into Jim's thigh in an upward motion. It would have gone in all the way to the hilt but Dole punched the side of her head hard with his fist. She dropped like a stone, unconscious.

Jim dropped the cuffs and was staggering back with a look of surprise and pain on his face. "Ackk! Damn it!"

Dole finally spoke. "Boss, you okay?"

"No I'm not okay! I told you to watch her!" He sat down hard and winced. The improvised dagger was sticking out of his right thigh with an ooze of blood spreading in his jeans around the blade.

The blond in the next cage had been watching this and started laughing. "Yeah. Get 'im good," she managed between bouts of hilarity.

Dole was looking from his boss to the laughing girl and back trying to figure out what to do next. Lyla still lay unconscious on the floor between them.

Jim looked up from the weapon in his leg and saw Dole's confusion. "Put her back in the cage with the handcuffs on and call the infirmary. I need some help before I can pull this thing out. Then get Frank to help you deliver the girl. The Boss won't like to be kept waiting." Dole stood there staring at Jim. "Well, get a move on!"

Finally, Dole bent and put the handcuffs on the girl, who he then scooped up and dropped inside the cage. She stirred slightly and moaned, then lay still again. After closing and locking the cage door, Dole quickly ran for the corner office.

Jim looked at the still-laughing blond and yelled, "Shut-up or you'll be next!"

She immediately became silent but continued to stare at him with mirth.

The other two guards in the warehouse were quickly walking toward their leader sitting on the floor.

"You guys get back to your posts!" he bellowed. They stopped, looked at each other, and slowly turned to obey, glancing over their shoulders from time to time as they walked.

Then Jim looked at the dark-haired girl lying on the floor of her cage. "Oh, boy," he muttered, "the Boss is gonna love this one."

Chapter 22

"If you see anything suspicious, speak up." Samuel was adjusting his console.

"I'm seeing a lot, and it's all suspicious," Joseph responded. Samuel, Joseph, and Curtis were traveling southwest on old Highway 59.

They had all received the mental commands from The Traveler. Immediately preparing for the task, they had suited up and ran for their assigned MASS tank, the same one in which they had brought Bill to the headquarters. It had been re-supplied and stood ready near the double-door entrance.

The tank now jostled over the small sand dunes that had crept over the road. Curtis sat in the driver's seat. They had left the old city limits and were in the open country southwest of Houston. The brush wasn't as thick here as it was further south, and there were even open grasslands. All sensors were on maximum range, but the targets of their search could not be picked out on any of the screens. Two men on foot, armed, and carrying a large radio. Samuel was concerned at the high number of feedback readings they were getting on the wildlife. Every rabbit, rat, and raccoon was showing up as a red blob. "Adjust sensors to show only masses over 100 pounds. That should get rid of some of this stuff."

"Yes, sir." Joseph adjusted a dial on the instrument panel and then entered some commands on a keyboard. The computer responded with two beeps and the screens instantly cleared. Then slowly some blobs re-appeared. A group of five lay dead ahead at about a distance of a mile.

"Switch to camera for that group. Telephoto." Joseph flipped a switch and one of the screens changed. A group of grazing deer came into view. There were more than five, but the smaller ones didn't show up through the filter. "Keep searching."

* * *

Fred and Jose were in a clearing in the brush, several yards from the road. They had stopped for a rest and a quick bite of the food they had stolen from the farmer's wife. They had been moving through the brush as much as possible, keeping off the road but still following it. Since the brush was beginning to thin now, it wasn't as hard to do.

Fred was finishing up his food with some water from a canteen when he thought he heard a noise. "Did you hear that?"

"What?"

"I don't know, sounded like something big, kinda far off—a rumble. Thunder, maybe?"

Jose listened for a moment. "Naw, I dint hear nothing. You better call in, it's been a while."

"That it has." He reached for the mike on the backpack he had taken off before resting. Switching on the radio, he said, "Base, this is Scout One."

There was static, then very weakly, "Scout One, this is base, read you weak and garbled."

He spoke a little louder. "Base, we are continuing on same route, nothing to report."

"Copy, Scout One. Continuing as ordered."

"Scout One out." He switched off the radio and replaced the mike. "Well, fun time's over. Let's go."

* * *

The female computer voice activated. "Intercepted radio transmission copied. Line of bearing established at two-zero-five degrees true."

Samuel sat up. "Play back the message." Joseph typed in a command and they heard the voice of the bandit loud and clear.

"Base, this is Scout One." The reply was garbled, but as they listened to the closer transmission, they looked at each other.

After the message completed, Samuel said, "Try to clean up the other end." Joseph adjusted some controls, but replay after replay didn't make it any clearer.

75

"Well, at least we have a target."

Curtis said, "That bearing puts them almost dead ahead."

Samuel turned to Curtis, "Open her up. Let's go!

Chapter 23

Bill sat in the single seat of the Kronos. It was very comfortable, more so than the seat in the tank had been, but this one had multiple control panels that could be brought in front of him on arms attached to the sides of the chair's single post support. Some had screens on them, some had keyboards and number pads, and others had joysticks and toggles. They all stored neatly at the sides, but it was very puzzling to look at. Russell sensed his confusion.

"Don't worry, William. I will talk you through each of these controls when the time comes. They will soon become familiar to you."

"If you say so." It was fairly noisy in the ship, and he had to speak loudly. But he could hear Russell perfectly in his head.

"I do. Over here we have food storage, disposal, water spigots, a shower, and a toilet. No need for privacy, as you will be alone—at least physically. I will always be only a thought away. Now, in most space travel, you would have to worry about being weightless. But that won't be a problem in this ship."

"What do you mean by weightless?"

"Exactly that. You would weigh nothing and would float around the ship, as would everything else not tied down."

"Sounds interesting."

"Oh, it would be very enjoyable, and for one small part of the trip you will experience it. But for the majority of your journey, you will feel the opposite effect. You will, in fact, be heavier."

"Why's that?"

"You will be constantly accelerating or, in the last half of the trip, decelerating. In other words, speeding up or slowing down. Only at the halfway point will you feel weightless, when the ship turns around. You see, you will be shielded from the gravity well in front of the ship, so as the ship falls into it, it will constantly accelerate…building tremendous speed. But the acceleration will give you the sense that you are pressed toward the floor a little more than you are right now. It will take some getting used to, but in eight weeks you will be stronger. And hopefully a little healthier."

"Healthier? You mean…?"

"Yes. You have a cancer of the bones. But as your body realizes it needs bones even more to support your additional weight, it should fight the cancer—an added benefit."

Bill thought about this for a moment. "And I'll be stronger because everything else is heavier, too."

"Very good! Yes, even lifting a cup of water will become exercise. And when you arrive on Earth in the past, everything—including your body—will seem as light as a feather."

"Swell." He thought some more about this. "Exactly how far back am I going?"

"That, my dear William, is *the* question, isn't it? I'm afraid I will have to tell you later, while you're on your trip. For now, I have a surprise for you that I think you'll enjoy—and it may give you answers to some of your questions. Follow me."

They departed the ship and walked in a different direction than they had come. Some of the workers paused to watch them go. They all knew the importance of the success of this mission and were working hard to make sure everything was just right, carrying some of the confidence their leader had imparted on them. Bill caught sight of them looking at him and nodded a greeting, which they returned with smiles.

Russell saw this and as they walked he said, "You're quite the celebrity, you know."

"The what?"

"They all know about you. I have told them about you, and you are our hero."

"You mean like in a storybook?" Bill was having trouble understanding. "Why would you tell them such a thing?"

"Oh, only because it's true."

"No, it's not."

"You are going to do something to save the world, aren't you?"

"Well, I don't know. Am I? Because you won't tell me a damn thing, and it's getting kind of frustrating."

Russell chuckled again. "But don't you see? I've been telling you things all morning, and some of it has been overwhelming. If I tell you everything at once, you will have a much harder time understanding. Trust me. All will be revealed in due time."

After continuing a little further in silence, they stopped in front of a rather large building.

Russell said, "If you will follow me in here, you will see something you've probably never seen before, even though our predecessors used to do this a lot. We found this equipment in Houston and set it up here. This is something they used to call a 'movie theater.' It is where stories come alive in moving pictures on a large screen."

"Yeah, my mom talked about these. She said that's where she and dad used to go sometimes."

"Well, William, you are about to enjoy something the world hasn't seen in a while. And it will be educational as well. I want you to pay particular attention to the way the people interact—the way they dress. Pay attention to what they enjoy and don't enjoy. They lived in a very different world than we live in today, but it is important that you fit in with them, do you understand?"

"You mean…I'm going to go…"

"Yes. This movie is from the time not too long before the war. Now, they are waiting for us inside. Oh, and William?"

"Yeah?"

"While you're paying attention to all the things I told you to, don't forget to enjoy the story as well."

Chapter 24

Lyla moaned and stirred on the bed. Ramey watched her with hungry anticipation. She had been brought in by Dole and Frank earlier with an explanation of what had happened. The story was hilarious to Ramey. Dole had told him he needn't worry, she had been thoroughly searched for more weapons, but none had been found. Ramey deduced that she had constructed the knife from the junk within reach of the cage and told them to make sure this didn't happen again. He added a lethal and unpleasant threat to make sure.

Ramey was alone with her now and smiled as he watched her from a chair near the bed. She stirred again and her eyes fluttered open. She looked around, bewildered, as she started to sit up. Then the pain in her head made her stop. She closed her eyes tightly and lay back down.

Ramey spoke. "How are you feeling?" His deep voice was genial enough.

She moaned again and asked, "Where am I?"

"You're in my recreation room."

She opened her eyes once more and half rose on her elbows, looking around. There were harnesses hanging from the ceiling, tables with straps, and the walls were lined with various devices of torture. Then she looked at Ramey. She had never seen him before, and as she saw his caveman-like features, she screamed. He began laughing, which shut her up. She glanced at the room full of devices again, then at Ramey, as realization quickly dawned on her face. Fear was replaced with terror.

"You can scream all you want, and you will be screaming a lot, soon. I heard you stabbed one of my guards. Very nice. I like a girl with some fight in her. They usually last longer."

"You go to hell!" she hissed.

"Oh, you'll join me there in a moment. But first, take off your clothes.

Slowly."

"Fuck you!"

"Yes, we'll get to that, too. Now if you don't take them off, I will." Suddenly she felt an invisible force tug at her flannel shirt. She grabbed it with both hands across her chest, but the fabric began to rip. Soon it left her body and its tatters were flung across the room. The skirt quickly followed. She curled up naked on the bed and began to cry.

"That's better. Now we can have some fun. Or at least…I can." She felt herself being raised off the bed and floating through the air. She thrashed about, trying to fight whatever was doing this to her, to no avail. She drifted slowly to a table, and as she settled on it, the straps wrapped around her arms and legs, holding her spread-eagle. She began to scream again, and this time she didn't stop for a long, long time.

* * *

Craig could hear the woman's screams down the hall. He had heard them many times before and knew his master was enjoying himself. He tried not to think about the girl or any family she might have had. Such thoughts were dangerous. They would get you killed around The Boss.

Then he heard another sound from the other way down the hall. Someone was running toward his office. Soon the communications operator appeared in his doorway, out of breath and excited about something.

Breathlessly he said, "Word from the scouts…they've spotted a tank."

"Tell them to stay clear of that thing! We don't know the range, but they're deadly. You heard the briefing from the Boss!"

"Yes, sir. I relayed the instructions as I was told to. They're staying as far from it as possible."

"Good. Keep me updated on any new information as soon as it happens. I'll inform The Boss when he comes out. If we want to live, we won't disturb him right now."

"Yes, sir." The operator hesitated and looked down the hall toward the screaming in the rec room. A look of disgust crossed his face briefly. Then he turned and ran back toward the comm center.

Chapter 25

"Stop on that ridge, near the cliff. We'll try to get another reading."

Samuel had seen a lot of blobs in the distance ahead on his screen and thought two of them had to be the targets. They had heard the intercepted transmission to the adversarial base and knew they had been spotted. The MASS tank stopped on the edge of a cliff overlooking a broad flat valley that ran in an east-west direction. The cliff edge was roughly fifty feet above a sloping, boulder-strewn base that led to the valley floor, which stretched a few hundred yards to the other side. The vegetation in the valley was thicker due to the water from the creek that flowed through it. The road dipped between cut-out cliffs on their left and descended into the valley. The cutouts were made at a ninety-degree angle to the natural cliff. The tank was on the western corner surrounded on two sides by sheer drop-offs, but it had a commanding view of the valley. There were quite a few blobs in the valley and beyond. Any of them could be the targets.

"Large biomass detected, west-northwest," the female voice on the computer informed them.

Samuel widened the field of view on his screen and faced the sensors to the right. A huge group of blobs was making its way slowly toward them.

"Switching to camera," he said.

At first they could only see a large dust cloud, then as the camera zoomed in on its base they could make out a large herd of mixed animals. There were bison and cattle, some of which were abnormally large and deformed. They were moving along peaceably enough, grazing on the dried grasses that had grown among the sparse trees and prickly pear cactus. But something had made them a little nervous, and they were staying close together instead of their normal spread-out herding pattern.

Samuel said, "Must have been a buffalo ranch around here in the past. They got out and multiplied, mixed with the cattle. Narrow the filters to anything between one hundred and three hundred pounds. Switching back to infrared." This cleared out most of the large herd, except for some calves, but left most of the original blobs in the valley and beyond. "Watch for two moving together."

* * *

Fred and Jose were crouched behind a rock across the valley from the tank. They had stopped again and surveyed the valley from the ridge on their side— always a good idea to look ahead before moving, at least when the opportunity presented itself, and this time it paid off. They had seen the tank approaching in the distance and had radioed it in. Now they were watching it after it had stopped on the cliff's edge.

"Look over there." Fred pointed to their left across the valley. A dust cloud was clearly visible, but it was difficult to see what was making it. Fred raised his binoculars. "Sweet Jesus, would you look at that."

"What is that?"

"That, my friend, is a herd of buffalo…and some cattle mixed in too, I think. I've never seen anything like it."

"Gimme the glasses." Jose took them and looked at the herd. "Aye Dios mio," he said softly. Then he looked back at the tank, which had stopped for now. "I think they're looking for us."

Fred then reached for the mike on the radio, which Jose was carrying for now. He switched it on and said, "Base, this is Scout One." They heard static, then a garbled response they couldn't understand. "Base, I can't read you but will transmit anyway. Enemy tank has stopped its approach. We may have been detected. We are staying put to observe. Scout One out." He replaced the mike and switched off the radio without waiting for a reply. He looked again at the herd. "That must have been what I heard earlier…and it gives me an idea. But we gotta hurry."

"What are we doing? You told them we were staying here."

"Just follow me, but stay at least a hundred yards behind me. Remember what The Boss said about those tanks? They have some kind of sensors that can see warm animals through the brush. So try to move like an animal, OK? But

I'm moving fast, so try to keep up."

"Got it. Can you move like a deer, vato? 'Cause I can."

"Whatever. Just keep up."

Fred took off along the ridge to the west. He soon found his way to the valley floor, with Jose following. They moved quickly, but erratically, running in spurts and stopping, much the way spooked deer will do.

* * *

"Radio transmission copied. Bearing one-eight-five true."

"Play it back." After they heard the message, Samuel said, "All right, look for stationary readings within line-of-sight. And don't worry, nothing they can carry will hurt this tank."

* * *

Fred had made his way across the valley and up a notch in the cliff toward the back of the herd. They were grazing along the ridge between him and the tank. He was waiting behind another rock for Jose to catch up, watching the animals. There were around three hundred of them, some of them huge and with legs growing out of their backs or with extra horns. One of the bison stood about twelve feet high at the shoulder but was remarkably well-formed otherwise. Their hooves stirred up dust as they moved and the cloud drifted over the valley.

Soon Jose crouched next to him, panting and exhausted. Fred looked at him. "Deer don't sound like that when they run."

"Chut up, bastardo!"

"Shhhh! I don't want to spook the herd. Not yet anyway. Do you still have that old grenade with you?"

Jose looked at him, puzzled, then looked at the herd. Slowly a smile spread across his face.

* * *

"Anything?" Samuel was getting frustrated.

Joseph continued flipping switches and turning knobs. "Nothing stationary. A lot of deer and wild hogs out there. All within the parameters. Never seen so much wildlife in one area. Must be this valley and the creek running through it. I keep switching to camera, but everything's moving or stopping only to graze."

They all heard a loud bang some distance from the tank.

The computer calmly spoke. "Explosion detected. Biomass approaching rapidly."

"Put cameras on that herd!" Samuel yelled. The screens filled with approaching bison and cattle, wide-eyed and panicked. The edges of the cliffs were funneling them toward the tank. "Shit! Start firing at them!!"

"Battle mode one," the computer said as they tried to quickly warm up the laser ball. But it was too late. The tank rocked as the first beasts slammed into it. Their bellows could be heard as they crowded and pushed on the vehicle. Many of them kept running right over the cliffs on either side of the tank.

The giant bison plowed through the herd, knocking several more of the others over the cliff. It spotted the tank with its silver ball rising and became enraged, perceiving this as the threat to its herd. It lowered its head and charged. When it made contact, the armor buckled as it crushed a cow into the tank with its enormous skull. Its huge horns pierced the armor and tore into the electronics. It lifted with its powerful neck muscles, and the tank was pivoted up and stayed balanced on two wheels at the edge of the cliff for a second. The men inside instinctively held on to whatever they could, terror etched on their faces as circuits popped and smoke filled the cabin.

Once again, the computer spoke calmly, but with a distorted voice, "Roll danger, tank unbalanced, please correct." When it seemed like the tank might come back down, the bison, which had backed off for a second charge, slammed forward and pushed the underside with his head lowered again. Its horns caught on the maze of tubing that ran the inside length of the vehicle's bottom. This time it pushed the tank's wheels off the edge and it fell. The bison couldn't stop, as its horns were tangled, and it was pulled by the tank. Its huge hooves skidded off the edge as well. The connected giants plummeted and tumbled down the cliff, smashing into the rocks below.

Chapter 26

"That was...amazing!" Bill was walking from the theater with Russell after viewing the movie. He was talking rapidly and was too excited to attempt hiding his limp. "They all had so much free time to just sit around and talk. It was all so clean. And the food!"

"Yes. Looked delicious, didn't it?"

"You said it!" He stopped and looked at Russell, his expression changing to one of concern. "That's the way it's supposed to be, isn't it?"

Russell stopped and regarded at Bill with a pleased look on his face. "I knew I chose the right person. Yes, William. That is the way most of the world should be. There will still be turmoil, wars, and strife. But nothing like what we have now. If we do nothing, mankind will only last a few more years, and then...well, the Earth will go on without us. Eventually the land will heal and life will continue, but something very precious will have been lost. Remember those other civilizations I talked about? The ones who gave us this technology?"

"Yes."

"They think we're worth saving...and that's why they're helping us. Some day we will be able to go and play in the rest of the galaxy like they do now. Some day we will all have my abilities and even look like me. Some of us will even come back and visit our former selves in this time."

Bill started them walking again. "Okay, I think I'm startin' to get it now. You're sending me back in time to fix something...to prevent the war. Right?"

"Yes."

"But what if I mess up? What if I do something wrong and the war happens anyway?"

"Then we are all lost. And that's exactly what would happen if we did nothing. But don't worry, William, I have every confidence in you."

"At least somebody does. Because I'm not so sure." Russell stopped and looked at him. Looked *into* him for a few seconds.

Bill was starting to get uncomfortable. "What?"

Russell finally spoke, "William I wish I had time to help you with your self-confidence. You have some issues with your past that won't let you believe in yourself. I could help you face them and overcome them. I'm not going to lie to you, it wouldn't always be pleasant. But you would emerge a more capable man, and you would even stop having those nightmares."

"How…how did you know about those? I haven't told anyone!"

Russell just smiled and tapped the side of his enormous head. Suddenly he stopped smiling and his face went blank for a few seconds. "Oh, my."

"What? What is it?"

"It would seem the bandit scouts have destroyed one of our tanks."

"What? How?"

"It should have been a simple task to stop them, but they are very resourceful. I'm afraid I need to take care of this. You go ahead to your room and have some lunch. Then there's another movie for you to watch. You know the way. Don't worry, William. The mission will go on."

Bill watched him hurry away down a side street. He thought about what Russell had told him—something in his past. For the life of him, he couldn't think of anything that would affect his sense of self-worth. He knew he was pretty useless at everything except killing bandits. *That* he could do just fine. Russell should send him after those scouts. Then he thought again about the movie he had just watched. All those people seemed so…*happy*. They thought their problems were so big, but they were nothing. *Must be nice.* He turned and headed back to his room.

Chapter 27

"Holy chit! Did you see that?" Jose was ecstatic.

"Yeah. Worked like a charm," said Fred. "Let's go down and check out that tank."

Most of the remaining herd had reversed direction from the cliff and were running north. The two men made their way down the notch in the cliff and walked along the base of the slope at the bottom. When they reached the place where the tank had come to rest, they could hear some of the electronics still popping in the rubble. The mangled body of the huge bison lay next to the tank. Strangely enough, the distorted female voice of the computer was still talking.

"Malfunction detected…breach of nuclear core detected…recommend immediate evacuation…danger of radiation exposure imminent…" It repeated the messages over and over.

Upon hearing the voice, both men drew revolvers. They approached the wreckage cautiously but saw no movement. The battered door had popped open, and the tank was now on its roof. Both men looked inside at the occupants. Their seats had broken loose, but their destroyed bodies were still strapped into them, obviously dead. They re-holstered their weapons and walked toward the road. The slope above them at the base of the cliff and the road itself were strewn with dead and dying cattle and bison. They cut a couple of back-steaks from one of the dead calves and packed the meat away for later that night.

"Man, I haven't eaten so good in a long time," Jose remarked.

"Tell me about it. I think we could take our time out here. If we weren't being watched, that is." He motioned toward the sky.

Jose looked up nervously. "You think he watches us all the time? I mean, everything?"

"Don't know. I just know he *knows* things. And I'm not gonna piss him off if

I don't have to. But he did say he couldn't follow us in here. I'm sure that weird wall back there had something to do with it. I have a feeling someone else is watching us now though."

"Yeah, that's right. You felt it, too. When we came through."

The two men moved off the road when they reached the top of the slope and back out into the sparse brush. After trying the radio again and getting nothing but static, Fred made the decision to abandon the heavy piece of equipment. They relayed to base what had happened in case they could be heard, and then hid it in the brush. Continuing to follow the road from a distance, they skirted around the occasional towns they encountered. One of them was burning enthusiastically, as was the eventual fate of most of the ghost towns. There were any number of ways for the fires to start, and no one was there to put them out, so they cheerfully gobbled everything in their path until there was nothing left to consume. The two scouts stopped along a river and camped in a clearing centered in a copse of trees, building their own fire and cooking the meat.

After eating their fill, they lay next to the small fire and waited for sleep. Fred said, "You know, if this other guy—The Boss's brother—is watching us, he's not gonna like the fact that we beat the shit out of one of his tanks."

"Yeah. You think he's gonna send more?"

"I would. In fact, if he can watch us like The Boss, he can probably tell them where to go. I'm kinda surprised he hasn't already attacked us. We need to be extra careful from here on out. We better sleep in shifts...I'll take the first watch." He got up and moved a little distance from the fire, looking out at the darkness between the trees.

Jose looked around and moved his rifle closer to his makeshift bed and then slowly closed his eyes.

* * *

In the early light of the next morning, Jose sat with his back to the fire. He had long since lost his battle to stay awake but was still sitting in a slumped position. Fred was curled up near the fire, sleeping on his side.

The soldiers had the small camp surrounded and were watching the two sleeping men. Their jumpsuits were brown camouflage, blending them in perfectly with the east Texas winter surroundings. Jake Gilder, the lieutenant in charge, gave a signal with his hand. Silently the other four men in the squad emerged from the trees and approached the camp, rifles aimed at the two men. Their instructions were to take the men alive, if possible, and return them to HQ. Trained in stealth techniques, they easily entered the camp and carefully removed the rifles and pistols from the oblivious scouts. Then one of the soldiers looked into a handheld infrared sensor and turned slowly around the camp. He looked up at Jake and nodded.

Jake gave another signal, and the soldiers slowly backed out of the camp. When they reached the edge of the trees, he loudly cleared his throat. Both men jumped and reached for their rifles, which were no longer there. Then, as if choreographed, they simultaneously reached for their pistols—also not there. They looked around and saw the soldiers with their own rifles trained on them. Jose glanced fearfully at Fred, who had already accepted the capture. He looked back at Jose with not a little contempt.

"Gentlemen, my name is Jake. I have orders for your capture and return to Headquarters. However, if you don't cooperate I will not hesitate to kill you immediately. Am I understood?"

Fred looked at Jake and then the other soldiers but said nothing.

"Am I understood?" Jake repeated calmly. Still there was no response. He signaled the soldiers and they kneeled and aimed as if steadying for a shot. This had the desired effect.

Jose blurted, "Jes! I understand!" He raised his hands. Although it seemed impossible, Fred looked at him with even more contempt. Then he slowly raised his hands as well.

Chapter 28

Ramey sat at a table in the rec-room and ate ravenously. He was a little surprised to hear a hesitant knock at the door. Ramey usually despised being disturbed when he was at breakfast, but he was in a good mood following his day of torture with the young girl.

His last act had been to rape her mangled body and choke her to death during a climactic finale, and then he had fallen asleep next to her remains on the bed.

During his breakfast, he enjoyed glancing at the lifeless form and smiling at the memories he had created the afternoon and evening before. The good mood carried into his voice, "Come in!"

Craig opened the door slowly, expecting to be killed instantly for the usually taboo interruption. "Boss?"

"Craig! My trusty companion! How are you this fine morning?"

"Good, sir. I'm terribly sorry for the intrusion."

"Well, usually I wouldn't allow it, but I had such a good time with the girl you provided. You will take care of her for me, won't you? I mean before she starts to stink up the place."

"Of course. But first I have an urgent bit of news. The scouts haven't reported in for several hours."

"Several hours—how long exactly?"

"Since yesterday afternoon."

Ramey's face froze. Slowly it went from pleasant to anything but. "Yesterday afternoon," he repeated slowly, enunciating every syllable.

Quickly Craig added, "Your orders were to not be disturbed while..." he indicated the dead girl on the bed.

Ramey's face softened a little. "Yes. But perhaps you don't understand, my friend, how important this operation is. My brother is hiding something.

Something big that will probably destroy us all. Now, what do you think I care about more? Hmm?"

Craig looked around the room frantically, as if to find an answer. Finally he looked directly at The Boss and steadied himself. "You would have killed me," he said quietly.

Ramey froze again. This time his face reversed direction from the last time. Soon he began to chuckle. This grew into a laugh that became quite boisterous. Craig began to smile in spite of his uncertainty as to where this sudden change was leading.

After his laughter died down, Ramey looked at Craig with genuine affection. "You are absolutely right, my old friend. I most definitely would have. So, they haven't checked in since yesterday. What was their last transmission?"

At that Craig brightened. "We could hear them, though it was quite garbled, but they couldn't hear us. They said they had destroyed one of the tanks."

"What? How?"

"With a herd of buffalo."

"A herd of buffalo?" Ramey thought this over for a moment. "Damn, I would have loved to have seen that."

"They said they got the herd to stampede, and it pushed the tank over a cliff."

Ramey thought for another moment and started laughing again. "Oh, to have seen my brother's face at that one!" He got up from the table and paced around the room deep in thought. Finally he stopped and looked at Craig. "But they were damn fools. I gave them orders to stay away from those tanks. All right, the time of waiting is over. Gather up all the troops and tanks we have ready. We leave at dawn tomorrow."

This shocked Craig. "But sir, we need more time! They're not prepared!"

"Well, get them prepared. My brother is likely going to capture those scouts, and when he does he'll know everything they know. And they think we're not going to attack yet. If we're going to have the element of surprise, we need to move now."

Chapter 29

"**B**eautiful, isn't it?" Ellen appeared at Bill's side, seemingly out of nowhere. He was standing in the courtyard watching the final prep work before the test launch. The party was going on around them, and there was a great deal of drinking, laughter, and loud voices. It appeared the whole town had shown up. Russell was mingling with the technicians near the craft.

"Yes." He turned to look at her and smiled. "I just hope it will work. I'm not too keen on getting killed, just yet."

Ellen returned his smile. "I'm sure you have nothing to worry about. Our engineers are well trained, and their motivation is clear. We all know what's at stake."

That last made Bill a little uncomfortable. "Yeah. I guess I need to be careful. I just wish I knew what I was going to be doing."

She looked at him again, more serious this time. "I know, it's frustrating. But it's best to not know too far in advance so you don't have so many preconceived notions."

"Uhhh…sure."

Ellen smiled again. "Okay, it's like this. If Russell told you everything you were going to do now, you would have a lot of time to think about it. You could eventually change your mind about some things, raise a lot of questions about what you were doing, and so on. Russell has thought this out very thoroughly, and he knows exactly what you must do. So it's best if he tells you just beforehand and then you do it. It's the only way to be sure the plan works. Do you understand?"

Bill thought for a moment. "I think so. I just hope I can do what he asks. It's the not knowing that's gettin' to me."

"Don't worry. He has every confidence in you, and won't ask you to do anything you can't do."

"Funny, he told me the same thing. Well, that's some comfort, I guess. I—"

At that moment an amplified voice boomed over the noise of the party. "Ladies and gentlemen, may I have your attention, please?" The partiers quieted down. "We're moments away from the test launch, and I need everyone to step back behind the red lines on the floor for your own safety." The crowd complied and spread to the edges of the courtyard. "Our test pilot is Chief Engineer Antonio Perez." Raucous applause erupted from the crowd as Antonio ran up the ramp and stopped at the top to turn and face the group with his arms raised. He was a middle-aged man with salt-and-pepper hair and a matching beard, wearing a bright red jumpsuit with emblems sewn onto the shoulders. A microphone on a long cord was passed to him.

The somewhat intoxicated crowd quieted again. "Folks, we've been waiting for this moment for a long time. And I for one am glad to say it's finally here!" There was another burst of applause. "I would like to go through the list of people who are responsible for making this happen, but I would be up here all day!" Laughter and more applause filled the air. "Suffice it to say, building this craft has been a labor of love. But we mustn't forget that we lost some good men along the way." The group remained silent. Bill glanced at Ellen, who was on the verge of tearing up. He decided now was not the time to ask. "I'm sure they are with us in spirit today. But as we remember them and the hard work of many, many others, let's also remember why we're here today. We have been given an opportunity to right what was wrong. And I'm glad to see we are celebrating this event. We should celebrate it. Because if we did this right, and I'm sure we did, we are going to save mankind!" This time the applause and yelling was thunderous. Many of the group turned to look at Bill and nodded approvingly. He smiled shyly and nodded back. After a while, the noise died down, and Antonio said, "And now, a few words from our leader!" Again, the crowd applauded.

Russell, in his usual white jumpsuit, moved his small frame up the ramp. There was no need for a microphone. He looked out and smiled at the audience as he began to speak telepathically. "Friends, Antonio was right about everything he said, and I thank him." There was even more applause. "We shall soon see the fruits of our labor realized. But first I have an announcement to

94

make. As most of you know, we lost a tank and three good soldiers yesterday to the bandits." Angry murmuring came from the crowd. "But I assure you, their deaths shall not be for nothing. Our own commando unit has captured the two bandits responsible this very morning." The murmuring turned to applause and loud cheering. "They are being brought in as we speak and are almost here. I need for you all to avoid the prisoners when they arrive. I will interrogate them thoroughly, I assure you." More questions arose in Bill's mind. Russell looked at him, and instantly Bill received the idea that the small leader would dig deeply into their minds and not at all gently. He found himself smiling at this.

"Now, to the matter at hand. Let's see this beautiful ship in action!" More deafening roars came from the crowd. Russell stepped down the ramp and made his way toward the technicians, where he sat in a control chair. Antonio waved to the audience and stepped inside the ship. Attendants walked up the ramp to make last-minute adjustments and to make sure Antonio was properly strapped in. After the last attendant had left the ramp, Antonio flipped a switch, and the two halves of the door on the Kronos swung closed. Bill watched as the attendants walked to one side of the room and joined other technicians where there were several control panels installed, covered with hundreds of dials, knobs, and meters. They all sat in chairs that were bolted to the floor and strapped themselves in.

The amplified voice sounded again. Bill could now see it was one of the technicians seated at a panel and wearing a headset. "All clear the launch area. Activate main doors."

The huge doors at the peak of the hill began to split apart slowly, allowing bright daylight into the underground facility. A few small clouds could be seen in the blue sky beyond, and a shaft of sunlight fell on one of the buildings. There was a good breeze blowing, and some dried grass and dust fell into the hole in the top of the hill, drifting lazily toward the ship and facility floor.

"Start main engines." The ship began to hum, almost imperceptibly at first. Then a series of lights on the outside of the ship came on.

"Commence count-down." Another voice came on, counting off seconds backwards from ten. At seven seconds, a very strange thing happened. A clump of dried grass stopped its downward movement and seemed to hover above the ship for a moment. Then it reversed its direction and picked up speed, quickly

95

shooting out the hole where it had entered, followed by other clumps and dust. At five seconds, Bill could feel a strange pull toward the ship and had to lean back a little as it grew stronger. The crowd also felt it and began to murmur loudly again. They were all leaning back, and it appeared they would fall, but they didn't.

When the countdown reached zero, a quiet hiss could be heard as the ship levitated off the pad. Everyone was silent and seemed to be holding their breath. The ship had risen about two feet, and then another sound could be heard over the hum of the craft: a muffled clank from inside. Instantly the pull toward the ship vanished, and most of the crowd fell on their behinds. The ship stopped moving upward and started to fall back on the pad. Instead of hitting the pad, it stopped and hovered for a moment and then slowly settled back down. Bill could see Russell with his arms stretched toward the ship, and he knew the little man was holding it and not letting it fall. The landing gear creaked slightly, and the engines could be heard winding down. Technicians were running up the ramp as the door opened again. Antonio came storming out, his face almost as red as his jumpsuit.

Bill walked over to Russell, who remained calm as the technicians swarmed over the ship and control panels. He asked, "What happened?"

Russell looked at him and said, "Remember I told you that the future is uncertain? Well, I did not see this happening. It's a way of making life more interesting. Imagine if I knew everything that was going to happen before it happened. Do you know how boring that would be? No surprises like this one. Sometime between my visiting the future and now, someone changed something, probably something very small. This small change affected the outcome of the test flight. But that is why we have test flights, to work out the bugs. I can see you are worried, William."

He looked at Russell. "Well, shouldn't I be?"

"I'm sure we'll find what caused this and fix it, though I'm not sure how long it will take. Meanwhile, why don't you go to your room and relax."

Bill thought for a moment and said, "If it's all the same to you, I'd like to stay and watch for a while."

Chapter 30

Fred sat in his cell thinking. They had brought him in with a cloth sack over his head and in chains until he got here, as he assumed they had done with Jose. He had no idea where his partner was, but he hoped Jose wasn't telling them anything. He also knew there wasn't much chance of that happening. Jose understood the consequences if they ever got back to The Boss.

Fred looked around at his cell; three white walls and a set of white bars for the fourth: about ten feet by ten feet with no windows. A sink, the small cot on which he sat, and a toilet, which he hadn't quite figured out how to use, were the only fixtures. Everything was white. There was no apparent source of light, but he could see everything clearly. The floor and walls seemed to be concrete, the bars solid. Even his clothes and boots had been taken, and he was now in a white jumpsuit like all these other idiots—and nothing else.

He got up and padded to the bars on his bare feet, trying again to see where he was. There was a single hallway leading off to the left, but he couldn't see where it ended, or anything else for that matter. Only a smooth white wall.

"Hey!" he yelled. His cry went unanswered and seemed to be muffled somehow, as if the walls didn't echo. This added a feeling of closeness that he found uncomfortable, and he decided not to yell again.

He went back to his bunk to wait some more because it didn't seem he had anything else to do. As he sat down on the end of the cot, he heard a voice.

"Hello, Frederick."

It came from inside his head. He froze and waited.

The voice continued. "I am Russell, the leader here. I'm speaking to you telepathically, which means I'm speaking directly to your mind."

"What the hell do you mean? Where are you?"

"I just want you to know that I will be taking all your knowledge and making it my own. This will not be pleasant for you, but I am not doing it out of spite. I simply need it for our survival, and this is the quickest way. I believe you have been heavily influenced by my brother, the one you call 'The Boss.' All of your people have been misled into thinking you must take from anyone you can in order to survive. But that will only lead to destruction for everyone."

Fred was looking around his cell, still trying to find the source of the voice. "Yeah...uhhh...whatever you say."

"You won't find me. I'm elsewhere in the facility." He continued. "You have been living a life of cruelty under my brother, so you won't be too surprised at what I'm about to do. I want you to know that I won't enjoy it either. Since you have been taking for so long, it seems I need to take something back from you, as I have already taken it from your friend.

Fred received a mental image of Jose lying on his cot with a blank expression on his face, some foamy drool leaking from his mouth and soaking the pillow. He seemed dead except for his ragged breathing. Fred was so shocked by this vision, he didn't even register how he had gotten it.

"What did you do to him?!"

"The same thing I'm about to do to you, I'm afraid. I could just ask you questions, but I really don't think we can trust you to be completely truthful, can we?"

"You can go fuck yourself."

"Yes, I thought so. But don't worry. When I am done with you I will know everything you know. If there are any worthwhile ends you need tied up—anything ethical, that is—I will be sure to accomplish them for you."

"As I said before, you can go—"

"Yes, I heard you. Very well, I will begin."

The pain was immediate and intense. Fred grabbed his head and fell back on the cot screaming as images from his childhood were brought up and ripped from him. He writhed in agony as his entire life was shown to him like moving pictures, one after the other, then roughly pulled from his mind leaving something like bloody stumps behind. Images of living in The Boss's compound and attending briefings were lingered over slightly longer before they were torn away. Memories of things like raping and killing women and children were also pulled away.

After what seemed like an eternity to Fred, he was released. Actually, the whole thing had taken under four minutes, but Russell had left one memory behind for him: the memory of the agony he had just endured. It was the same thing he had done with Jose. This one memory had given him something to hold onto, painful as it was, and he was still conscious but dazed.

Russell spoke to him. "I have decided to leave you with us, for now. You can still have your memories, although they can only be accessed through this event, so you may not want them. Your knowledge of my brother's plans is very useful to us, and you may be of use as well in the upcoming days. If for some reason our mission fails, you will be rehabilitated to become a useful member of our society. But for now I will leave you."

Fred lay on his cot with his feet still on the floor and stared at nothing. His mind couldn't find anything to hold onto but what it had just endured, and touching that only brought back the pain. He decided to float in emptiness for now, not aware of himself or where he was. Maybe later he would go back and check on that one thing and maybe it wouldn't hurt so much, but not now.

For now, it was much better floating in the emptiness—just floating.

Chapter 31

The line of tanks was interspersed with infantry and supply trucks as the convoy left Laredo. Ramey was in the turret of the lead tank. He had modified some goggles to fit his oversized brow and was wearing them to keep the dust out of his eyes. A few scouts on horses trotted ahead of the convoy to radio back major obstacles, and the limestone dust they kicked up blew back over his tank. The day was already warm as the sun shined to their right, just over the horizon.

"Scout to convoy," the radio crackled, "Looks like a bridge out ahead, moving up to investigate." The scout horses broke into a run.

"Of course there's a bridge out, I told them that," Ramey grumbled. Then to Craig, who was driving the tank, he said, "Keep going. They're going to find we can go to the right of the bridge and traverse the wash. It's not going to get rough until we go around that settlement and cross those rivers."

The convoy plodded on toward his brother's headquarters far ahead. At this speed and traveling constantly, they would probably reach the wall in a couple of days. Ramey had traveled this pathway without his body several times and had briefed them extensively on it, but the idiots seemed to find every obstacle and head straight for it.

"Scout to convoy, looks like we can traverse the wash if we keep right."

Ramey sighed in frustration and keyed the mike on the radio, "Gosh, do you think so? Check your damn maps and look ahead a little or I'll have your nuts for lunch. You got that?"

"Yes, sir!" came the quick reply.

"I swear, I don't know if it's even worth it," Ramey mumbled to himself.

The convoy crossed the wash with no problem and by noon was within five miles of the settlement. Ramey ordered them to turn north-northeast, per the maps, and to travel cross-country for a while. They were to eat on the move and sleep in shifts in the tanks or trucks as they traveled. He suspected his brother had gotten into the heads of the original scouts and would be expecting him a few weeks from now. He couldn't wait to see the look on Russell's face when he got through the wall in physical form. He would quickly go outside his body and find his brother, relish the surprise on his face, clean his clock, and return to the convoy to get them moving again.

He had briefed his army that there was to be radio silence during this portion of the trip and absolutely no gunfire. The crew had been taking potshots at wildlife on the way and had even managed to bag a large deer, which was passed to the chow truck. At one point, the scouts had come upon a pack of peccaries, which had scattered and spooked the horses. One of the steeds had managed to buck off a scout, who fell on a mesquite log and broke some ribs. He had been replaced and patched up, now riding in a troop truck with a small bottle of corn liquor for the pain. This proved to be a mistake because another enterprising soldier "fell" out of the same truck in an attempt to get some rest and alcohol. Ramey, who had to halt the convoy each time, quickly killed the man with a look and asked if anyone else wanted to give it a try. Of course, the men remained ardently quiet.

Now was the tough part. Even though the tanks could push through most of the brush with no problem, there was the occasional grove of mesquite to contend with. These trees had wood as hard as iron and a root system that resisted even the most persuasive attempts to push them over. At some points they had to stop the convoy and hack through with axes and saws, which delayed progress by hours, mainly because the cutting tools required constant re-sharpening.

Fortunately the main rivers lay to the north, so they did not have to be dealt with just yet. As the small army worked its way through the treacherous land throughout the afternoon and into the night, some of the men began to quietly question why they didn't just push through the town where the old road ran. But they knew better than to question their leader on the matter and toiled on.

As one group approached a particularly large mesquite and began to work on it, a strange low buzzing began to emanate from inside it. A quick investigation of the tree revealed it was hollow with a large opening on the far side. A soldier carrying an oil lamp got on his hands and knees and peered inside—and was immediately bitten on his face by an enormous rattlesnake. The rest of the group backed up to watch the soldier die rather quickly but painfully as his face and neck turned purple-black and swelled. Another soldier found a long stick and fashioned a metal hook onto the end. He probed into the still-buzzing tree and managed to pull out the creature, which turned out to be sixteen feet long, almost eight inches thick, and very, very angry. It had gone into the tree to digest a half-grown wild pig it had eaten, and there was a large bulge halfway down its length. The men managed to pin its head to the ground and quickly hacked the snake up. Since it did not seem to be deformed, other than its size, it too was passed on to the chow truck.

While they were waiting to get through the trees, Craig approached Ramey. "Boss, I've heard some of the men complaining about going around that settlement. They think it would make nice practice for our tanks to blow the hell out of the place."

"Yes I know what they're thinking. But if they get one whiff of us out here, they'll radio back and there goes our element of surprise. Got it?"

"Of course. I'll inform the men."

"You do that. And one other thing…tell the chef to cook me up some of that snake right now. I'm hungry and this is going to be a long night."

Chapter 32

The monitor on the wall showed a peaceful scene. It was familiar to Bill and he was enjoying the serenity of it while he sipped his herbal tea. He had eaten a hearty breakfast of eggs and some sort of cured meat wrapped in a tortilla with a side of salsa. While he had eaten he watched the monitor, as he often did, for signs of bandit trouble. But as always there was none.

The village could be seen from the hilltop where the outpost was hidden, and the women were preparing the meal for the camp. Some of the men had already left for hunting before the sun came up, and others were working in the winter gardens. The children were helping out or playing nearby. The lookout posts on the walls were abandoned.

Also from the monitor came the sounds of radio chatter between the sentry tanks. "This is post one, report."

"Post two, all clear."

"Post three, all clear."

"Copy. Keep sensors at max range. Perform pre-maintenance checklist by next report. Post one out."

It was the same almost every time. Good. The last thing he needed was to find out they had been attacked again without him there. Not that the three tanks couldn't handle it better than he could, but it would still be a serious distraction for him. He left the monitor running and turned his attention to the schematics of the Kronos. He had requested them and they were now spread over the desk in his room. Most of the stuff was way over his head, but he pored over it anyway. He tried to concentrate on the control panel drawings, but the words were foreign to him. He found he couldn't stop yawning when he tried to make sense of the drawings, even though the tea was supposed to be stimulating. They were putting him to sleep.

Suddenly the monitor on the wall switched off.

Bill looked up at it quizzically when he heard, "Hello, William."

"Oh, hey."

"Would you please come to the Kronos. There's something I want you to see."

"Sure, be right there." He got up and put the tea cup on the table with the rest of the dishes. Walking out of his room and toward the center of the underground city, he returned the friendly smiles and greetings of the people he encountered along the way. It was a little strange to see so many happy people in one place, but he supposed they had it pretty nice here. Why not be happy? Still he felt a little skeptical, and something kept him from giving in to the warmth he felt here. He supposed years of living in miserable conditions will do that to a person.

"Yes, and it would take years of living in these conditions for you to be completely comfortable here."

Bill stopped and looked around, bewildered. "What, how…?"

"I'm sorry, William. I was listening to your thoughts without your permission. But believe me, I would never betray them to anyone. Oh, and I can see what you're thinking of me right now. Don't worry, you won't hurt my feelings—ever. I am your friend, whether you believe it or not. I have seen some of the worst thoughts mankind has to offer, and yours are quite tame by comparison. I'm afraid the monitoring of your thoughts will be very necessary in the time to come for me to help you. I'm sending you into a strange new environment that can become hostile very quickly, and that would be detrimental to the mission. You will see that it will come in very handy at times."

"Yeah, if we can ever get the ship off the ground," Bill said as he continued walking.

"Yes, that is what I wanted to show you. We will continue when you arrive at the Kronos."

Bill rounded a corner and saw that workers were again crawling over the ship, checking connections and making repairs where necessary. Russell was standing in the doorway and motioning for Bill to come inside. When he climbed the ramp, he was met with the same warm greetings from the workers. Once inside, he followed the small leader to an area behind the control chair.

"I wanted you to see that we found the cause of the problem," Russell continued in his head. "Do you see that cable coupling?" On the wall where Russell was indicating were attached several thick black insulated cables. At different intervals they were connected by shiny silver sleeves, which appeared to be the couplings he was talking about. One of them had come loose and the cables were hanging with exposed connectors inside the ends. "This wall was not properly shielded from the gravity well, and the cable was pulled upward and became uncoupled. These cables are the main power conduits from the generators to the engines. Engine two lost its power and the computer immediately shut down the other three to avoid having the ship tear itself apart. Of course, had I not been here, that's exactly what would have happened when it fell.

"You see, one of the workers adjusted the shields slightly and they were off some. That's what happened after I went to the future to watch the test flight. I didn't catch it, and the future changed from what I saw."

"Well, that's comforting," Bill said sarcastically.

Russell chuckled in his head. "Actually, the engines shutting off is a safety feature that is built in. If this had happened in space, you wouldn't have even known anything was wrong if not for the alarm indicators…and of course you would instantly become weightless when the ship stopped accelerating. It was an easy fix, and the gravity shield has been adjusted again. We are going over the ship very carefully to avoid another mishap and should have another test run in a day or so."

"Is this going to affect your mission?"

Russell looked at him, "My mission? This is *our* mission, William, and do not forget that. The fate of the human race will soon rest in your capable hands. We are assisting you by putting you there, but you must carry out the mission in the end. Do you understand?"

Bill thought for a moment and then nodded.

"And to answer your question, no. We are sending you back decades in time, so a few days one way or the other can be easily compensated by adjusting your speed and trajectory. The onboard computer is very precise." Russell indicated the control panel in front of the chair. "It will fly the ship for you and keep you alive. And it is sensitive to my thoughts as well, so it will follow my commands if adjustments are necessary. That is why your training needs are minimal."

"Well, believe it or not, that is comforting to know. I was starting to get a little worried looking over those schematics."

Russell chuckled again. "Yes, I sensed that. Don't worry about the complexity of this ship. You will be more passenger than pilot. The computer and I will fly it for you."

"Sounds like I won't have much to do during the trip."

"Oh, don't worry about that either. I will keep you occupied."

Chapter 33

The convoy had worked through the night and by mid morning had reached the old highway traveling northeast from the village. From there it was much easier, with only a few river crossings and downed bridges to worry about. But the rivers were shallow and fairly easy to forge. By late that evening they were approaching the wall. Ramey knew the area from his out-of-body attempts to breach it. Just before they reached the marked place in the road, he halted the lead tank.

"This is it," he said to Craig. "Make sure nobody moves toward where I'm working until I give the word."

"Yes, sir."

Ramey dismounted the tank and started forward. He could sense the wall ahead and approached it tentatively. When he was standing inches from it, he stopped and took a deep breath. Then he pushed through it as fast as he could and immediately sat down cross-legged on the other side. He had practiced for this moment for some time now and worked quickly, leaving his body and zooming straight toward where he could sense his brother.

* * *

Russell was startled from his sleep. He immediately knew his brother had broken through the wall by using his body and was now in the room with him. Ramey instantly reached into his mind and tried to destroy the part that was creating the wall, but Russell's reaction time was quick and he struggled to stop him, sensing what he was trying to do. The skirmish went on for some time, and Russell was tiring quickly, especially after holding the wall up for so long. Then again, Ramey had a great deal more practice destroying minds than did Russell. Eventually Russell succumbed, and Ramey crushed that part of his brother's mind. The invisible wall fell away and the road was now clear for the convoy.

Russell pushed his brother from his mind and managed to keep him from destroying anything else. Ramey tried again and again but couldn't get in.

"Ha!" Ramey said, "at least I got your stupid wall!"

Russell tried to probe Ramey's mind, but he didn't know where his body was. He knew it must be somewhere along the wall perimeter, but where?

"Doesn't matter. Apparently I don't need it anymore. What are you doing here?" It was a moot question.

"Well, brother, you have managed to keep me out for a long time. It's high time I take a look around." There was nothing Russell could do to stop him. His large head hurt from the struggle, and he was weak. Instead of trying to stop his brother, he put an immediate invalidation on Bill and the Kronos. At least he could still do that. Ramey would not see him or the craft or take any interest in them if he did. The invalidation field spread throughout the compound and no one's mind would place any importance on Bill or the mission. Ramey would mainly be looking for defenses anyway. Russell thought quickly about what to do next. This was another one of life's surprises that he had not anticipated— and not a good one at all.

When Ramey returned, he said smugly, "You don't have this place very well defended, brother. Well hidden, but not defended. Maybe you depended on your wall a little too much."

"Yes, apparently so. But your abilities here are limited, and I won't let you do any more damage."

"We'll see about that." And suddenly he was gone.

Russell didn't take time to follow him but immediately sent messages to his engineers to prep the ship. Then he woke up Bill.

"William. This is Russell. Wake up immediately." He gave him a gentle shake telekinetically.

Bill jumped to his feet and looked around, bewildered. "What?"

"You must leave immediately. My brother has breached the wall and—wait a second…" Russell quickly left the compound and, now that his brother had re-joined his own body, he could locate him a hundred miles southwest. He looked the situation over and returned. "…he's got a convoy of tanks and trucks. There's still some time, and our tanks will hold them for a while, but he may get through. You *must* leave immediately. Quickly go to the Kronos. It is almost ready for departure."

"Um…okay. On my way."

Bill was already in a jumpsuit, which he had put on after his shower a few hours before. He looked around the room but didn't see anything he wanted to take with him. Out the door he went and broke into a fast, limping trot toward the Kronos. There were others running in the same direction, and he quickened his step.

When he arrived, there was a flurry of activity. Checklists were being run, and there was a cacophony of normal and loudspeaker voices. Through it all he heard, "William, I am almost there. Go immediately inside and sit in the control chair."

Bill trotted up the ramp, and Antonio was there beckoning him inside. "We're almost ready for lift-off, Bill. How are you feeling?"

"Well, I just woke up…"

"Yes, we were all taken by surprise. But are you feeling all right otherwise?"

"Yes."

"Good. Have a seat." Bill complied, and Antonio buckled him in. The chair was set in a somewhat reclined position and was very comfortable. "You're going to feel some strange sensations as the engines rev up. The shielding and the gravity well have to sync up, so you may feel lighter and heavier in intervals. Don't worry, that's normal. The repairs have been made and, uh…it will work fine now." His tone betrayed his confidence.

"You don't sound so sure."

"Well, one can't be certain about everything. I mean, it should have worked perfectly last time. But that's how life goes, no?"

"Yeah, I suppose." Bill was working to hide his own fear. He had to remind himself that this was all to save the world—that something he would do soon would somehow prevent the awful war and the horrible aftermath.

"All right," Antonio said, forcing a smile. "We will leave you now and seal the ship." He held out his hand. When Bill shook it, he said, "God speed and God bless, my friend."

"Yeah. Thanks."

With that he turned, and the other workers followed him out. The door whirred until it clanked shut. There was a hiss, and Bill's ears hurt for a second as the air pressure changed. An internal speaker came on, and he heard the same voice as in the MASS tank. "Vessel sealed, pressure nominal," the soothing and somewhat familiar female voice reported. Bill looked around the ship's interior as if seeing it for the first time. The controls were sparse. A button panel could be swung up in front of him, but he saw no need to do anything but sit tight. The monitor in front of him was black. "Engine sequence initiated." Bill heard and felt the engines come on and gripped the handles of the chair.

Suddenly the monitor switched on, and Russell's familiar face was on the screen. He was smiling. The voice in Bill's head said, "William, we're almost ready. Try to relax, there's nothing for you to do but enjoy the ride."

"Easy for you to say. I don't mind dying, but I'd like it to be quick if that's all right with you."

Russell chuckled. "I'll talk you through everything that's going on. And I won't lie or hide anything from you about this ship and its systems. Right now everything's working perfectly."

The computer voice sounded again. "Generator speed nominal, switching to internal power." The lights flickered and became brighter. "Gravity well engines online." There was a change in the humming of the engines as they took on a load. He felt himself become lighter, as if he were being drawn toward the ceiling, then he gently sank back into the seat.

"That was weird," he said to anyone who was listening.

Russell said, "Yes, interesting sensation, isn't it?" Bill looked out the portholes and saw the workers strapped into their chairs, which were bolted to the floor. They appeared to be hanging in their seats as their hair and clothes were drawn up. He could see Russell's small body on the monitor straining against the shoulder harness. "You're going to feel some acceleration now. The clamps are about to be released."

Bill had heard nothing of the outside announcements as he had heard during the test run. He hoped they had remembered to open the doors in the roof. With a metallic pop, he was pressed further into the seat as the Kronos left the ground. He saw movements in all the portholes as the ship rose smoothly and accelerated toward the underside of the hill.

Chapter 34

Ramey sped back to his body and stood up, a little unsteady from his mental battle with his brother. After a moment, he stood straight and looked at Craig.

"Mount up! Move 'em out!" Those at the front of the convoy had seen him push through some invisible force and sit down, but when he walked back to the lead tank the force had obviously vanished. Craig quickly gave the signal and the convoy began moving forward on the road.

* * *

Bill was finally close enough to the underside of the hill to see the open doors through the upper portholes. The black sky beyond looked ominous. He looked down and saw the rooftops of the buildings growing distant below him. He was high enough now that a fall would surely kill him. To no one he said, "Well, I guess this is it."

"Don't worry William, I will not let harm come to you." Russell's voice was reassuring.

The ship continued to accelerate and soon passed through the doors. The blackness through the portholes was complete until the interior lights dimmed dramatically. When his eyes adjusted, he could see stars above and almost nothing below. He had no idea how high he was now, but through one of the lower portholes, he saw what appeared to be a line of lights in the distance. Russell spoke again. "That's my brother's convoy heading toward us. MASS tanks have been dispatched, and we have planned for this contingency. Do not worry about us."

"If you say so."

"I do. I'm only sorry you had to take off at night. I wanted you to enjoy the breathtaking view from this altitude. You will soon be out of the atmosphere, and the computer will swing the ship around toward the lit side of the Earth."

* * *

Below, Ramey felt a twinge of something and looked up as his lead tank plodded through the night. Something was there, and then gone. No matter. He was mentally preparing himself for the battle that lay ahead.

* * *

Bill remembered the sight Russell had showed him in his mind only days before—the beauty of the Earth so far below him. It was beginning to get noisy inside the ship. He felt the craft rock a little, as if crossing over a bumpy road. "What was that?" he asked, a little alarmed.

"Just some atmospheric turbulence," Russell said. "You are traveling quite fast now—faster than anyone has traveled in a long time. Since air is relatively light, it is not affected by the gravity well very much and doesn't get out of the way." Shortly, the bumpiness abruptly stopped. "There, you have broken the sound barrier. It should be a fairly smooth ride from now on. The air will get thinner until it disappears."

He noticed that the roar of the wind was becoming less. "But how will I breathe?"

"Just like you are doing right now. You have been breathing recycled air since we sealed you in. The beings I visited thought of everything when they passed me this technology. You have everything you need to survive the harshness of space." The Kronos creaked and popped as it continued to accelerate upward. Russell anticipated Bill's next question. "That is just the ship adjusting to the lower pressure outside. Completely normal."

After a while the ship seemed to stop moving, and all Bill could hear was the hum of the engines, although he was still pressed into his seat. He looked around at the portholes, and in one direction, he could see a line of pink. It was slightly curved.

"William, my friend, you are in space." Russell seemed elated. "That pink line is the southern horizon. You may unbuckle and move to a porthole for a better view." He did so, but his arms seemed incredibly heavy. He struggled to get out of the chair and fell to the floor, crawling sluggishly to the porthole where he managed to sit, mesmerized by the view. His head seemed too heavy and was difficult to keep steady. The line in the distance had widened and became mostly white. Soon it became an arc and started to grow at a rate that Bill could detect. After a while he was looking at a large half-circle that was visibly shrinking below him.

"Is that..."

"Yes, that is the Earth. You are above the South Pole. That large white landmass is the continent of Antarctica, surrounded by the blue ocean."

Bill was speechless.

"It is quite beautiful, isn't it?

"Yes, it is."

"Look to your left."

Bill did so and gasped. Through a side porthole he could see the moon, also a half-circle, which appeared to be suspended by invisible means against a background of brilliant stars.

"Remember this sight, William. You will see it again soon, but you cannot replace the feeling of seeing it for the first time. It would be a shame if you and I were the last people to see it. But then again, that is why you are on this mission." Bill watched as the huge ball below him shrank smaller and smaller.

"Now your acceleration rate will slow some." Quite suddenly, he began to feel lighter, though he still didn't feel like he did when he boarded. It nauseated him a little.

"There. This is how heavy you will feel for the rest of your journey. You are at one-point-two-five the normal force of Earth's gravity. I hadn't intended for you to have such a quick take-off, but my brother caused a change in our plans, and I had to get you out of here and away from him as quickly as possible. I am shielding your existence from him."

Bill thought about Russell's abilities and understood what his brother was capable of. "That's fine with me. So, now that I'm in space, what else can you tell me about the mission?"

Chapter 35

Ramey's tanks were refurbished from an Army that was the most advanced in the world during the war. But they were old now and had been subjected to decades of harsh weather. A few of them were lost along the way, but enough survived the trip for a decent battle, in Ramey's opinion. He couldn't wait to see how they would fare against his brother's fairytale weapons. The tanks were built for a crew of four, but lean times had often reduced the number to three, and sometimes two. The crews and ammunition from the lost tanks were dispersed among the remaining battle vehicles.

Ramey was still in the lead tank as the first signs of dawn approached. The only other occupants were the alternate driver and Craig, who had been trained to fire the weapons.

He turned to his second in command. "Keep the driver and the radio quiet. I'm going to check out where my brother has his ambush set up."

"He has an ambush?"

"Of course he does! Now let me concentrate." He sat on the tank floor, which was rocking from the rough road. He left his body and rose straight up to survey the land. It was light enough to see now, but there was no sign of his brother's tanks. *Wait*…about ten miles ahead there was a long, low hill with the tanks in a line spread out perpendicular to the road in the valley beyond. He approached to get a closer look. One of the tanks was in the valley on the nearer side of the hill. When the convoy approached up the road, this guy would signal the rest of them and they would come up on the ridge once the convoy was in the nearer valley, taking them from three sides in a pincer movement. *Not bad, brother.*

He decided to see how his tanks would do in a fight. He re-entered his body and stood crouching in the cramped tank. He turned to Craig. "Who is our best shot with a tank?"

"I am, sir." There was no arrogance in the statement; it was just a fact.

"Hmph. Okay, who's the second best?"

"Well…probably Jenkins."

"And where is his tank?"

He consulted a clipboard. "Third in line, sir."

"Not for long. Find a place to stop the convoy for breakfast and a quick pow-wow. Then his tank will take the lead." He relayed the situation to Craig and then told him his plan. "We'll send his tank into the valley alone to see what happens. The others won't attack a single tank and blow their cover."

"Brilliant, sir."

"Yeah, I know. Now let's stop and get some chow."

Chapter 36

Instead of telling Bill the mission, Russell told him some things about how the Kronos worked. "The water is recycled, as is the air. But there will always be some waste material, which will be ejected through the side of the ship. All this is done automatically. The food is stored in several places about the cabin, marked 'Food.'"

"Come to think of it, I am a little hungry." Bill had stopped watching the Earth when it was so small it seemed to blend in with the stars. He was still getting accustomed to his extra weight. Instead of weighing one hundred eighty pounds, he now weighed two twenty-five. "I don't know if I can do this."

"It will get easier over time. Just rest often and drink plenty of water. Your body will adjust."

He found a drawer marked "Water" and reached inside, pulling out a metal bottle. It felt like it was filled with lead. He took a sip and winced. "Even the water is heavy. It pours down my throat like rocks in a sack. How fast am I going now?"

"Very. It will still be days before you approach the speed of light, but you are traveling much faster now than any human ever has."

"Swell."

Bill struggled to get up and walked to a small food door in the wall. He opened it and inside were some frozen meals on thin plates, wrapped in clear plastic. He reached in and grabbed one. "Whew. Cold."

"Yes, they are frozen to keep them from spoiling. Remove the plastic and place it in the door marked "Oven.""

Bill looked around until he spotted the door on the opposite side of the ship. He moved across the floor, opened the door, and it was very warm inside. He unwrapped the meal and placed it in the compartment, avoiding touching the sides, which he could tell were very hot.

He closed the door and asked, "Now what?"

"Now you wait for a while until it warms up. Temperature regulation is one of the most difficult things we had to deal with while building this ship. The engines and gravity well generators build up a lot of heat energy that has to be dealt with. And there's nothing in space to cool them with. You could try to radiate the heat out, but that would be such a waste. Fortunately, my friends across the galaxy gave us an ingenious solution involving heat exchangers and recycling the energy. Otherwise, before long you might be looking like your meal is about to."

"Great." He opened the oven door and looked at his food. The frost was gone and it was starting to smell good.

"Once you have eaten, William, we will continue your education."

"What?"

"You are going to have to blend in with society and deal with situations so as not to call attention to yourself. I have recorded some programs into the computer and will call them up to your monitor. Don't worry, it will be fun."

"Can't wait."

Chapter 37

After breakfast and a briefing, the lone tank, with Jenkins at the gun and a driver named Harper at the controls, crested the hill and entered the valley.

Both Ramey and Russell were watching from above, sensing each other's presence. The physical form of Russell was present among the MASS tanks just over the crest of the ridge. His body had been sped out to the battlefront in an old dune buggy-like vehicle that had been modified for fast travel over most terrain. He was there to prevent his brother from using telekinetic energy on his MASS tanks, as he was sure his brother would prevent him from doing to the older tanks. He had discovered that the closer he was physically to the object he was trying to move, the easier it was to move—or to prevent being moved. His presence at this battle was vital. He had left Bill and joined his body just before it arrived.

As the old tank came into firing range of the MASS tank, it stopped. At least it was what they were taught was the firing range, according to the old and faded manuals found in some of the tanks. Limited practice had proved the manuals fairly accurate. The MASS tank's laser had already been armed, and it fired a solid blue beam at the turret of the older war machine for a couple of seconds. Inside, Harper said, "Oh, crap! They're shooting at us with the ray gun!"

"Don't worry, I don't notice anything." And Jenkins didn't, until he felt heat coming from the tanks forward armor and heard the metal popping. A glowing red spot appeared on the inside of the turret, and he cursed. "Time to light 'em up." He aimed the tank's main gun at the MASS tank and fired. The effect was devastating on the newer vehicle. It exploded in a massive fireball that mushroomed into the morning sky.

Immediately, Russell, who had moved inside the older tank when it had been fired upon to see what effect the laser would have, communicated telepathically to everyone in the MASS tank division. "Set lasers to fire for ten seconds at this point." He sent a mental image of the old tank with a crosshairs over the spot where the penetrating laser would hit the ammunition stores. He showed them from different angles so they would know how to aim in any situation. They all instantly knew just what to do.

Ramey had returned to his body and told an elated Craig, who was waiting out of sight with the rest of the convoy, how it had gone.

"Hot damn! This is going to be easier than I thought," Craig exclaimed.

"Shooting fish in a barrel. Let's go get 'em."

Craig got on the radio to the other tanks and relayed what had happened. Cheers could be heard throughout the convoy. He gave the command to start the attack.

A second MASS tank came over the ridge and stopped. It was still out of range for the older tank, but they aimed at it anyway. The laser ball deployed and a solid blue beam appeared again, this time at a different spot on the old tank. Jenkins, who had been euphoric over his previous victory, laughed at the feeble effort. But this beam didn't disappear. His laughter stopped when the glowing red spot on the tank wall quickly turned orange, then yellow-white, then blue as the beam pierced the armor. It went through his chest and hit the ammunition storage box behind him. The inside of the tank became an instant inferno as the powder ignited, killing the two men instantly. With a loud *whoomp!* the turret literally leapt into the air and somersaulted end over end as a gout of flame shot up from the tank. The turret stuck in the ground barrel first, looking like a large, smoking, somewhat-angled sign on a post, perhaps warning others of a similar fate.

Over the hill, the noise could barely be heard through the roar of the old tanks spreading out and moving up through the sparse vegetation. Believing they were invulnerable, they planned on charging the enemy, picking them off as they came in range.

Ramey had ordered his driver to hang back behind the line so he could watch the battle from the top of the hill. When the tanks in front reached the ridge, they began to stop. The radio crackled in Ramey's tank and a voice said, "Boss, you might want to come and look at this."

Ramey looked at Craig. "Stop the tank." Ramey quickly sat cross-legged on the floor. He had become more agile at leaving his body quickly, and in no time he was above the valley. Immediately he saw the tank with smoke and flame billowing from it. Somehow they had beaten it. He looked at the other side of the valley and saw the lone MASS tank. He sensed his brother there above it and questioned him.

"How did you do that?" His reply was a feeling of warm brotherly love that he knew and despised. "Stop that!"

Russell finally communicated with words full of humor and good cheer. "Oh, dear brother, you didn't think it was going to be *that* easy, did you?"

"Well, sort of. You just wait until I get my hands on you. Can't wait to pop that big ol' head off that skinny neck."

"I look forward to it. You know, you could turn around now. Save us both a lot of trouble."

"Uh-uh. I've seen your little city now, and I want it. Looks pretty cushy. Nice hiding place, too."

"I'm glad you like it, but it's not up for negotiations. Go now, and your people and equipment won't be harmed."

"Well, I didn't plan on negotiatin'. Unless you consider a bunch of blowed-up toys an even trade."

"I can see you are still hard-headed. And stupid. Bring on your tanks, if you must, but be warned. Whatever happens here today, I hold *you* responsible."

Chapter 38

Bill sat in his chair and watched as the movie ended. It was a comedy, and he hadn't gotten most of the jokes, but it was still entertaining. He had a hard time believing these people took so much for granted. There were so many creature comforts that they expected and seemed to think somebody owed them.

He got up and went to the toilet. The increased gravity made everything difficult and tiring. Everything felt heavy—and seemed to hang lower. When he was done, he sat on the floor near a porthole. The Earth could no longer be seen, and the Sun was now just a bright star among millions of others. He could detect no movement but knew he was still accelerating.

Russell hadn't spoken to him in a while and he figured the little man would contact him when he was ready. He got up and went back to the seat, mounting it with some difficulty. The soft cushions felt good as he settled in. With minimal movements, he brought the screen in front of him again and thought about starting another movie. Then he decided to explore the other features. There was a pointer he moved with a little joystick, and he had several options to choose from. Movies, books, games, history, sociology, and one marked "Kronos." He moved the pointer there and clicked the button on the panel.

Immediately an animated schematic of the ship appeared. At the bottom was, "ALL SYSTEMS NOMINAL." He moved the pointer around, and little labels popped up when he moved it over certain parts of the ship: Engines, Gravity Well Generators, Gravity Shields, Radiation Shield Generators, Captain's Chair, Food Stores, Water Stores, Recycling Filters, Water Closet, Heat Exchangers, etc. He picked one at random and clicked the button. A short paragraph popped up.

"Radiation Shield Generators—During space travel away from Earth's general area, dangerous radiation levels may occur which would be harmful to human occupants. Sensors on the ship detect incoming radioactive energy, and the Radiation Shield Generators emit a magnetic field to divert the radiation."

Bill read the words but really didn't understand them. He decided to try another one.

"Water Stores—Water for consumption, bathing, and waste removal is stored here after passing through the filters. It is 99% pure with trace minerals for flavor, and contains no microbial life forms."

Well, that was comforting. Bill could remember drinking from ponds where some of the critters in it might swim up and bite him as he drank. He didn't know what "microbial" meant, but he didn't want any life forms in his water. He went through the other sections, learning a little more about the ship with each one. Some of them had animations to illustrate points. Slowly he became more confident that the ship was well-built by people who knew what they were doing. He could do without the constant heaviness, though. His muscles and joints were beginning to ache, especially his hip and right shoulder.

Bill decided to take his mind off the pain with a game. He closed the schematic and clicked on the "Games" button. Another menu popped up with different categories: Card Games, Shooting Games, Adventure Games, and Educational Games. He hadn't really played a game since he was a child, except for some cards with the other villagers. Upon opening the card games there were more choices. Solitaire, Poker, Gin Rummy, Bridge, and Hearts. His mother had taught him to play Solitaire one night after his chores were done. He clicked it and an animated deck of cards came into view, shuffling itself. Bill smiled. It took him a minute or two to get the hang of it, but pretty soon he was lost in a world of trying to beat "Ol' Sol," grinning away the whole time. *Yeah*, he thought, *maybe this isn't so bad.*

Chapter 39

The battle raged on for several hours. Each side had difficulty hitting a moving target, so both sides tried to keep their tanks moving as much as possible. Ramey's tanks, which were more numerous, fired and missed quite often. They soon found that the armor-piercing bullets were ineffective, but the larger shells were devastating. Russell's MASS tanks were putting burn scars on their targets, but doing little damage unless the older tanks stopped to aim. Eventually they found that if they aimed at the tracks on the older tanks, they could force them to stop, or at least slow down. On two occasions, Ramey's tanks accidentally fired on their own in the confusion, helping to even the odds.

Eventually, there were only two tanks left on the battlefield, one from each side. They circled each other, firing shots when they could. Russell and Ramey were watching from above the valley, their bodies safely sitting on the other side of the surrounding ridges in their respective rear tanks.

Russell said, "Well, brother, looks like we were pretty evenly matched after all."

Ramey said nothing, just sent waves of hatred. He had been trying alternately to crush and to levitate the MASS tank, but Russell wasn't allowing it.

Russell spoke again, "We could just call it a draw and go home. We've both lost a lot of good men today."

Finally Ramey answered. "Never. I won't stop until you're dead and your little underground village is mine."

"I was afraid of that." Then Russell sent a message to the MASS tank driver to retreat over the ridge to join the tank containing his body. As he predicted, the old tank pursued. Ramey tried desperately to send a mental message to the driver to stop without destroying his mind, but couldn't quite seem to get through to the idiot. When it topped the ridge, both MASS tanks fired and it quickly exploded before getting another shot off.

"Okay, brother. Now it's two against one. Do you surrender?"

But Ramey was quickly going back to his body in the last tank. He opened his eyes and told Craig, "Get us out of here! *Now!*" Craig nodded and revved the engine, turning the tank in a tight circle, crashing it through the sparse brush in retreat.

Then Ramey got another idea. "Wait. Stop for a second." Craig did, and Ramey opened the hatch. Climbing out of the tank, he said, "Go, don't stop until you're back with the convoy and get them the hell out of here." With that he slammed the hatch, jumped down and ran through the brush, lateral to the tank's direction. Craig guessed that battle had gone badly, though he hadn't seen any of it. He revved the engine again and was off.

Russell had returned to his body as well, and the two MASS tanks were in pursuit of the last bandit tank.

Ramey ran through the brush until he found a narrow wash and hunkered down under an overhang. Immediately he began to shut down all his senses and thoughts, hiding himself from his brother and only taking in information. After a few moments, he heard his brother's tanks crashing through the brush following the older tank. After another short while, in the distance he heard the humming of their weapons firing, and then he heard the old tank explode. Craig was dead. With any luck, his snotty brother would think he was dead as well. They would probably go after the convoy next, picking off the sitting ducks one at a time. That was okay. He could make his escape while they were busy. He meant what he said about not stopping until his brother was dead. This game wasn't over yet.

Chapter 40

Bill was sitting on the floor again, looking out a porthole. He was trying to eat some venison and mashed potatoes, but his appetite had been waning lately. Earlier, when his trip had begun, he was usually ravenous. The added weight of everything made him work harder just to move around. And he did notice some added girth to his arms and legs. His muscles were beginning to bulge.

Every time he woke from his sleep, which was unusually deep and mostly dreamless, he checked the timer on the screen in front of the chair. He had been out here over two weeks now. Russell had checked in on him regularly, answering questions and informing him how things were back home. He even provided him with a condensed mental replay of the battle, which was fascinating but gave him a headache. Bill had expressed happiness at winning the skirmish but quite a bit of distress at the high price paid in losses of Russell's people. Russell let him know that while the men would be missed terribly, each of them would gladly sacrifice themselves again if possible for this just cause. Russell had sent him mental images of the funeral ceremony, which was quite nice. Scores of women and children were crying at the losses of their men.

This only reinforced Bill's resolve to not let these people down.

While he was chewing the deer meat unenthusiastically, Russell spoke to him for the first time today. "Hello, William."

"Oh, hey. How's everything back on Earth?"

"Just fine. You, however, do not seem to be doing so well. I noticed your food intake has slowed. How are you feeling?"

"I'm okay. Just not real hungry. And my right shoulder is really hurting off and on."

"Hold on a moment...oh, I see."

"What?"

"It seems the added gravity of constant acceleration is not slowing the growth of your cancer after all."

Bill was silent for a moment and then said, "So what does that mean?"

"It means your pain will increase, unfortunately. There are some herbs packed in one of the food stores…here." He showed Bill mentally where they were. "Make a tea with some of this bark and it will ease the pain. Try to use it sparingly, and only when you really need to. It is quite strong. Hopefully you will complete the mission before the discomfort is too distressing."

"It's not hurting that bad right now. Hey, I noticed something about the stars."

"Yes?"

"Well, I like looking at 'em because they're beautiful and all. But after a while, they sort of just look the same day after day. Today, though, the ones out the bottom portholes look kind of redder than usual. And the ones up there," he pointed upward, "are kind of bluish. Why is that?"

"Well, William, that is because you are traveling so fast right now. You are approaching the speed of light, much faster than any human has gone before. The light you see from the stars behind you is being stretched, and the light from the stars ahead of you is being compressed."

"So what happens when I get to this 'speed of light' thing?"

"That's a very good question. I'm not really sure what to expect with the human body, but I was assured by my friends across the galaxy it is quite safe. As you approach the speed of light I suspect you will notice nothing, but your view out the portholes will change."

"What will I see?"

"The color shift will increase, and you will develop some tunnel vision. Only stars directly ahead of and behind you will be visible, and they will seem more crowded. And you will probably detect movement among them."

"You mean I'll be going so fast I can see the stars moving?"

"Yes, isn't that exciting?"

"Damn scary if you ask me. But I guess I have to trust you. Don't have much choice."

Russell chuckled amicably. "Don't worry, William. Remember, all our fates depend on this mission, so I won't let anything happen to you."

Bill was simultaneously distressed and comforted by this. "Okay."

"Beyond the speed of light, I'm not sure what you'll see. I will leave you for now, but I will always be listening. If you need anything, just call."

"Okay," he repeated.

"I encourage you to try some of the other games on the computer. They are quite imaginative."

"Sure. Soon as I finish eating. Don't be a stranger."

Russell chuckled again. "Oh, don't worry. I'm always around."

Chapter 41

Ramey was crouched behind a sage bush. He watched as the farmer's wife drew a bucket of water from the well and then went back inside the shack. Their garden was almost within reach, and the Sun had already set. He didn't dare steal food in daylight or he might catch a bullet from the angry occupants of the little shack. There were turnips and onions growing just on the other side of the sage bush he was hiding behind. Yes, they would make a fine dinner.

He had lived like this since running from the disastrous battle. Left on foot with only the clothes on his back, he'd had to fend for himself while he plotted revenge on his brother. He had traveled as close as he could get to the underground city and scouted it out. His heightened senses had saved him from tripping some of the many alarms around its perimeter, but he was beginning to see a way into the facility. He couldn't leave his body without his brother sensing him, so he was stuck finding a way in without that benefit.

He was almost always hungry and found it hard to kill game and cook it without being detected. Stealing vegetables was much safer. Sure, he could easily kill the farmer and his wife at this small farm he found in a remote area some five miles from the underground facility, but as soon as he started doing that, someone might miss them and go looking. He wondered why they didn't join the others in the city. They were probably aware of the city and vice versa. He was sure they were aware of the tanks patrolling the area, so he thought it might be a bad idea to kill them. Better for his plans to just lay low and steal a carrot now and then.

A couple of times he had run across others doing the same thing. If they made the mistake of challenging him, they would end up with a broken neck, or in one case worse when he discovered the challenger was female. Then he would have whatever they were carrying. In that way he had accumulated two knives, a small leather bag with a shoulder strap, some binoculars, and even a rusty old pistol with two bullets, not to mention a little more food.

His plan for dealing with his brother involved capturing one of the remaining MASS tanks when they went out on patrol, killing the occupants, and just driving right back into the hill, then finding his brother and wringing his scrawny little neck. Of course, he didn't quite know how he was going to sneak up on a vehicle with so many sensors and defenses yet, but that was just details.

He looked up at the shack and could see light coming from a window, but nothing else. He decided it was dark enough to make his move, especially with his stomach making hungry noises. He crawled from behind the bush and began pulling turnips. After his second one, he heard a growl that didn't come from his stomach. He froze and then slowly looked toward the shack. A large spotted dog had crawled halfway out from under the shack's porch and was staring at him, snarling. The low rumble from its throat could surely be heard from inside the shack as well. Ramey scrambled to his feet and began sprinting away from the shack, holding a turnip in each hand.

The dog began chasing him and was gaining ground fast as it barked loudly behind him. The farmer came out the front door with a rifle and yelled, "Hey!" He then shouldered the rifle and fired a shot at the retreating hulk of a man. Ramey *felt* the bullet buzz by, inches from his left ear. He began running an erratic pattern, trying to make himself a more difficult target as he made for some trees that would probably provide adequate cover. But the farmer must have felt he had gotten his point across because he didn't fire again. The dog, however, had a mind of its own and continued pursuit.

Ramey decided to take a chance on his brother detecting him and connected with the dog's feeble mind. Suddenly the dog saw a huge bear in its path and skidded to a halt, only a few yards behind Ramey. The bear growled and began running toward the dog, which turned tail and ran, yelping all the way to its protection back under the porch. He made the dog think the bear would be pacing around the shack for a long time. If he had killed the dog right-out, it would have angered the farmer, who would have then talked to his neighbors and possibly formed a posse. This way he was just a thief who got some turnips and had a puzzling effect on his dog.

Ramey ran until he reached the trees and then slowed to a walk as he entered their darkness. In the failing light, he found a large tree with a rock next to it and stopped. He forced himself to be absolutely quiet and listened. *Good.* Nothing could be heard but the hushed ruffling of some roosting birds overhead. Sitting on the rock, he brushed off as much dirt as possible from the turnips and began to eat while thinking about what had just happened. If his brother detected that little mind connection with the dog, he was done for. He decided he had better sit up all night here in this little copse of trees and keep watch. *Better safe than sorry. Or dead.*

Chapter 42

"**G**ood morning, William."

Bill woke from a fitful sleep and looked around at his now-too-familiar surroundings. He yawned and stretched, struggling to sit up in the increased gravity. After another yawn, he said, "Hey."

"I wouldn't have woken you, but something exciting is about to happen, and I need you to be awake for this."

"What? Is it time?"

"Yes. You are about to cross the threshold. Look out the portholes."

Bill looked up and could see the stars were completely blue and a little oblong near the edges of the complete darkness that flanked the ship through all the side portholes. The stars below looked the same way, but they were red. He could indeed see perceivable movement. It was slight, but it was there. "What's going to happen when I'm going faster than light?"

"Well, I'm not sure. My friends weren't very specific on that point. They are not human, you see, and don't even have eyes…at least not like ours. They sense their surroundings much differently than we do, so they couldn't tell me how you will experience this."

"Oh, great. So I may not even live through it?"

"I don't think that will be a problem."

"You don't think?"

"Well, I'm pretty sure you'll live through it. But I'm not sure how comfortable the experience will be."

"Oh, wonderful. So what can I expect—" Suddenly a brilliant light filled the ship, blinding him. "*Ah!*" He put his palms against his eyes. He also felt a slight lateral movement of the ship in the direction he was facing. This was accompanied by a slight creaking sound, as if the ship was adjusting itself again.

"What the hell was that?"

"You are now traveling faster than light. You should uncover your eyes." Russell's voice sounded different somehow…a little more distant and distorted.

Bill moved his hands from his face and opened his eyes. There were purple spots everywhere he looked, but they were slowly fading. Everything looked the same, except for the view out the portholes. The stars were gone. Nothing but complete blackness could be seen. "Where am I?"

"You are still traveling in the same direction, but you seem to have slipped into another dimension."

"Another what?"

"Dimension. It's as if you've punched a hole in space. You're sort of running alongside the universe right now. Don't worry, it's perfectly normal."

"Are you sure? You sound kind of funny."

Russell chuckled in his head. "As do you. How do you feel?"

Bill looked down at his body and ran his hands over his torso. "I feel fine, why?"

"Well, because you are also traveling back in time now. At least relative to the Earth and from my point of view."

"I don't get it."

"It's because of the direction you are traveling. This whole time you have been accelerating in the direction the Earth came from, relative to the center of the universe. While time on the ship has seemed normal to you, it has been slowing down on Earth, at least from your point of view. At the moment of that bright flash, time stopped on Earth, once again from your point of view. Now that you have crossed the threshold of light speed, it is moving backward on the Earth. It's a good thing you are in another dimension for now, because the Earth will catch up to you and pass you at one point, although you won't see it. It will continue to accelerate backward in time ahead of you and away from you, until you slow down below light speed, then it will start to move toward you again, but it will be years in the past on Earth. Of course, and I can't stress this enough, all of this is from your point of view. No one here has noticed anything. Do you understand?"

Bill thought for a moment. "I think I do. But how can you still talk to me if I'm going back in time?"

"Well, you're not actually going back in time, the Earth is—from your point of view. You're just traveling to meet it when it gets to the right date. And right now, I'm traveling along with you."

"Okay this is getting too complicated. I'm just going to have to trust you on this. But one more question, how do you know it will be the right time on Earth when I get there?"

"The ship's computers are programmed very precisely to keep you on this exact course and at the correct speeds. Don't worry. You will arrive at the right time."

"Can you at least tell me what the mission is now?"

"Not just yet. Please be patient, William, all will be revealed when the time comes."

"Yeah, yeah, whatever." He looked out the windows at the eerie blackness. If not for the perceived increased gravity, it would seem like he was sitting in a motionless room. He looked around the interior of the ship once again. "Should I expect any more excitement?"

"Unfortunately, no. It should pretty much be like this for a while."

"Okay. If you don't mind, I think I'll go back to sleep." He was starting to feel very groggy.

"Not at all. Good, uh, night I suppose, William."

"Yeah, g'night." He laid back down and closed his eyes, still seeing purple spots behind the lids. He fell almost immediately to sleep and began to have a very vivid dream.

Chapter 43

Bill awoke from his mattress on the floor in the two-room farmhouse, and sat up. The morning light was streaming in through the shuttered slats on the single window above the bed and made a rectangular beam of light that slanted through the dust in the air and across the small room. He followed the beam of light with his eyes until it came to rest on another mattress near the opposite wall. There lay the treasure of his life. Two twelve-year-old girls slept like angels. They were identical in every way—except to their loving parents, who could recognize them instantly as individual and vibrant souls. A soft sigh entered the air of the room, very close to him. He looked down and saw the beautiful mother of the two—yet another angel slumbering in the quiet morning. The scene was so peaceful and so devastatingly wonderful it made his heart ache.

The woman slowly opened her eyes and looked at him. Then she closed them again and smiled, snuggling deeper into the blankets. Only her dark hair remained visible on the pillow.

"You go make the tea," she said from under the covers.

He smiled and said, "You go make the tea," in a sarcastic imitation of her. Then he picked up his own pillow and dropped it on her head. Her giggles were muffled music to his ears. He jumped out of bed, wearing only some deer-skin shorts, and went barefoot into the other room, which served as the kitchen, dining room, family room, and just about everything else except the bedroom. He had already visited the outhouse during the night and didn't need to go again just yet. He opened the cast-iron stove and threw in some kindling and a couple of small mesquite logs. After he lit the fire, he looked in the water bucket. *Hmmm, empty.* He carried it over to the door and slipped on his moccasins. Looking through the slot in the door, he saw nothing stirring outside—nothing near the well or anywhere around it. He opened up and stepped out.

With his peripheral vision he saw the two men, one on either side of the door, a split-second too late. He heard the *thock* inside his head before he felt the pain, as one of the men hit him with some kind of club. His knees came unlocked, and he was falling down, down, never seeming to hit bottom. There was only blackness.

Then something peculiar happened. He felt himself lifting out of his own head, and then he was looking down at his body which was lying face-down in the dust. He heard quiet laughing and found that he could look around. The two men were standing over his body, smiling. They didn't see him floating here between them. He seemed to be a singularity—a mote of dust with a viewpoint.

One of the men whispered, "You didn't kill 'im did ya?"

The one holding the club, which resembled a miniature baseball bat, whispered back, "Naw, that was just a tap. But we better get to work. He'll be comin' around soon, and you know how The Boss likes 'em."

Bill watched as they dragged his limp body over to the chopping block in the yard about thirty feet from the side of the house. It was still face-down as one of the men placed his right arm on the block. Bill the dust mote watched in detached fascination as the other man took the axe out of a piece of wood nearby and hefted it in his hands. He smiled at the other man, who was still holding Bill's upper arm in place on the block. Then he raised the axe as if to bury the sharp edge into Bill's soft muscle and bone. The man holding the arm suddenly changed his expression to one of alarm. Upon seeing the desired response, the man wielding the axe stopped and grinned. Then he lowered the axe and spun it around in his hands so the sharp edge was facing up. He swung the axe hard and brought the blunt end down on Bill's upper arm. The crack was loud as his bone broke, but dust-mote-Bill didn't feel any of the pain. His unconscious body contorted and moaned and then went still again. The two men then repeated the act on each of his limbs, breaking his upper arms and his thighs—each time causing spasms and moans, but never awakening him—so that he would be completely incapacitated when he woke.

Dust-mote Bill was still watching all this…unable to have any control over any of it…and it all seemed very familiar. He knew he had broken all his limbs sometime in the past, but he couldn't remember when or how. He also knew he once had a wife and children but couldn't remember what had happened to them. Somehow he knew this was what had happened to them all, but the memories had eluded him for a long time now.

He watched as they sat his still unconscious body up against the chopping block. It would have appeared as if he were taking an early-morning nap if it were not for his misshapen limbs. The arms hung at odd angles, and the legs appeared to have one too many bends in them. After the men were satisfied he would not fall over, they turned to the brush-line about fifty yards from the small house. One of them waved his hands in a 'come here' motion. A couple of moments later six men quietly appeared and began stealthily trotting toward the house.

Suddenly, dust-mote Bill thought of his family inside. They were all still asleep and at the mercy of these brutal men. He found he could move in this form, anywhere he wanted to go. He quickly went through the wall to the bedroom and began screaming at his wife to get up. But there was no sound. He realized his mouth and lungs were still outside, part of his unconscious body.

The same two men who had so thoughtfully taken care of him were now inside the living area. They quietly crept toward the bedroom door. Bill tried to stop them by running into one of them, but found himself on the other side of the man's body. He was simply on one side, then the other. The men were still oblivious to his presence.

They continued to move toward the bedroom, and the one who had hit him stopped in the doorway. He looked in the room and saw the sleeping trio. Continuing on toward Bill's wife, he knelt down to the floor.

Still under the covers, she asked, "Is it ready?"

Not knowing what she was talking about, the man looked down at himself and then smiled. "Oh, it's ready, bitch."

Almost immediately, she threw off the covers and went for the rifle standing in the corner by the head of the bed, but the man was too fast. He grabbed her arm in his grubby hand, and Bill saw her wince in pain. With her free hand turned into a fist, she began to beat on the man while screaming, "Girls, *run!*"

They sat up in their bed and began rubbing their eyes, not quite awake. Their movements seemed synchronized, and it would have been incredibly cute if the situation weren't so tragic. When they opened their eyes and saw the strange man over their mother, they instantly became alert. Jumping up, still almost synchronized, they ran for the door where the other man was standing and smiling down at them. Bill saw that there was nothing friendly in that smile. They stopped, and in a snake like move the man had an arm from each girl in either of his hands. Their struggles were futile against his grip.

Bill watched as these men, obviously bandits, dragged his family out into the yard. They were all three struggling to get away and screaming at the men, who kept those hateful smiles on their faces. The one holding his wife nodded at the girls and said, "Tie 'em up." Other men who had been standing there watching the whole spectacle, some of them holding small coils of rope, began moving toward the captives.

Bill, who was becoming frantic in his realization that he could do nothing to stop this, tried to go back into his body. But it was like hitting a wall. He simply couldn't get through to revive himself. Eventually he accepted that he was a captive prisoner, doomed to watch the past replay itself.

He watched as the leader of these monsters arrived with his entourage. The man looked deformed, with a protruding brow and too much hair on his face and arms. He watched as they threw a bucket of water over his unconscious body—the same bucket he had been holding when they clubbed him—and the man he once was so many years ago finally woke up.

It took his old self a while to come to his senses and look around. When his eyes rested on his bound family, he jerked to get up and then screamed at the pain in his arms and legs. He lay there helpless as the men, about twenty of them now, laughed at his efforts to move. Dust-mote Bill watched as younger Bill tried to move slowly and only managed to fall from his sitting position to lying on the ground. The pain had been so intense he had passed out again. He watched as his wife cried in terror, in sympathy screaming his name, and in rage as she struggled against her constraints. His daughters simply cried and cried. The men sat his body back up and poured more water over him.

He awoke again and looked down at his useless limbs. He watched as the leader took his wife and stripped her naked in front of all the men and their daughters and began to rape her while watching broken Bill sitting there helpless. He saw the rage in his younger face and the determination to crawl toward his helpless and screaming wife. He actually made it about a third of the way before two men grabbed him and roughly put him back on his butt, leaning against the stump, making him pass out again. He watched as they splashed him awake yet again. When the leader finished with his wife, another man began to rape her, and the leader motioned the other men in. Some of the men even took turns with his daughters as he watched helplessly. His family's faces went from terror, to pain, and finally to catatonic shock. Broken Bill was also in shock, he noticed, now just sitting there with no expression on his face, staring at nothing.

Dust-mote Bill watched as his wife and daughters were killed with the same club they had used on him once everyone was through with them. His house was ransacked and lit on fire. The bodies of his family were thrown in through the burning door.

One of the men started toward broken Bill with the club when the leader stopped him and said, "Nah. Let him live with what he saw. He'll be dead before long, anyway." He watched as they walked away, some of them spitting on him as they passed by. Broken Bill just sat there, not reacting. His house continued to burn, and luckily for him the breeze blew the hot smoke away from his limp body.

Chapter 44

Bill woke again, feeling much heavier now, and tears were streaming down his face as he openly wept. He was racked with sobs while the still vivid images of his family being tortured and killed flashed through his mind.

"William, are you all right?"

Bill didn't answer, just sobbed loudly.

Russell waited patiently, and when Bill seemed to be getting control of himself, he repeated the question.

At first there was no response, then quietly, "No."

"What happened?"

"I saw...I *saw*!" he said and then began to sob again.

With this, Russell went carefully through Bill's mind. He saw the lucid images of what Bill had re-witnessed only moments before.

"Oh, I see."

He waited again while Bill recovered, and then he began to speak. "They told me this might happen. You see, traveling faster than the speed of light and entering the fourth dimension apparently has some strong side-effects on the mind, one of which you have just felt. There are things the mind binds up and stores hidden from us because they are too traumatic for us to face. We can't access them without other adverse effects, so they stay there, ever present and quietly affecting us, usually in bad ways. What has happened here in the fourth dimension is that one of these evil little bundles from your past has been dredged up and revealed to you."

He sat up in his reclined seat and swung his legs over the side. "Yes. It was in my past, wasn't it." Russell waited for Bill to struggle with something. Finally Bill began to speak through his tears. "I knew...something had happened to my family, but I couldn't remember what it was. All I remember is waking up in a room with a doctor working on me. He told me later they had found me near a burned-down building with both my arms and legs broken. He said I was in shock and almost dead. The man was a doctor before the war, and he knew how to set my bones so they would heal mostly the right way, but that's how I got this limp. He and his family just happened to be traveling nearby when they saw the smoke and came over to investigate. They put me on a stretcher and brought me to their settlement."

"Very fortunate for you."

"Yeah, but too late to save my—" the words were chocked off.

"William, I know you don't want to hear it, but this is actually a good thing."

Bill was instantly furious. He looked around the ship with its dark windows. "How can you say that?" he hissed through clenched teeth.

"Please, don't misunderstand. I don't mean what happened then was good, but it is very good that you remember it now."

"Why?" He was still angry, but his fury had lessened some. "I was doing just fine without knowing…that!"

"Tell me something, William. How do you feel right now?"

"I feel pretty damned pissed off is how I feel."

"How else?"

Bill thought for a moment and then slowly realized he did feel different—dramatically so. "I feel…lighter." He thought about it. "Like I've been carrying around this enormous weight that I didn't even know I was carrying. And now it's…well…gone somehow." Despite his tears, his face seemed filled with wonder.

"Yes. That's a very good way to put it. Anything else?"

Once again, Bill thought. "Yeah. I've often wondered where I got this hatred for the bandits, you know? I mean, obviously they're vermin and need to be killed, but I've really *hated* them to the point of hunting them down sometimes, just to kill them. It was as if doing that would somehow fix something that was busted inside me. Never did, though. And I never knew where that came from." He seemed to marvel at this new knowledge. "And now I…I do." He couldn't put his finger on it, but all this had made him feel better somehow. He was silent for a while and then slowly began to frown in thought.

"What's wrong, William?"

140

"I was just wonderin'; how can remembering the horrible thing that happened to my family...actually make me feel better?" He couldn't help but feel disgusted with himself.

"There's actually a good explanation for that. You've been carrying around that terrible burden of what happened for a long time. It's all been there in your mind hidden from you, making you feel angry and sad, making you feel hatred, but never revealing itself to you. Now that it's in the light for you to see, it can no longer do that to you. You are now free of its terrible influence, and that would make anyone feel better."

Bill had to think about that for a bit. Then a thought occurred to him. "Is this going to happen every time I go to sleep in this...whadayacallit...fourth dimension thing?"

"I'm not sure, but it is very possible. How do you feel about that?"

"Not too happy about going back to sleep."

Chapter 45

Ramey lay prone on the crest of a small ridge as he watched the MASS tank in the distance through the binoculars. He had been observing them for several days now, getting to know their patrol patterns. There weren't that many left after the battle, apparently.

"In about five seconds it's going to stop at that farm," he said to himself. He watched it approached the small farmhouse on a dirt road and slow to a stop.

"Now it's going to open up." Right on queue, the side of the tank opened, and a crewmember got out wearing his white jumpsuit. In the still morning air, Ramey could hear only some of the sounds at this distance. He barely heard the man clumping down the metal stairs of the tank's door ramp, but he heard nothing else until the man knocked loudly on the front door of the farmhouse. He heard the animated voices of an elderly woman who answered the door and the man in white as they exchanged pleasantries. The old woman was obviously hard of hearing, so the man was speaking loudly, but still Ramey couldn't make out any words. The man in white then retreated to the tank and disappeared inside, as the woman did the same into her house.

"Now he's going to give her a box of something and get a bag of something in return." Sure enough, the man in white exited the tank again, this time carrying a small metal box as he walked back to the front door. He stood there and waited patiently until it opened again and the exchange was made. She had given him a rather large gunny sack, probably filled with who knew what kind of vegetables, judging from the large garden behind the house, in return for the mystery box. Their voices were heard again as they hugged their goodbyes.

Yes, this would do nicely. The same routine could be seen every other day at the same time. Ramey watched as the tank continued down the road from the house and disappeared from view over a small rise. He then surveyed the small clump of trees and bushes directly across the road from the house where the tank stopped each time. It stood in a field next to a wooden fence holding a few cows. It was almost too perfect. Two mornings from now, he would pay the old lady a little visit.

Chapter 46

There were more dreams, but none as bad. Bill slept a lot in this dimension and sometimes didn't dream at all. He was growing accustomed to visiting his past and sorting out his distorted memories. He always awoke feeling better about himself and his life, and he had discussed this at length with Russell. However, he didn't feel any better about the increasing pain in his right shoulder and arm. Russell told him his cancer was growing.

During one of his dreamless sleeps he heard, "William, it's time to wake up."

Russell always knew just how to get Bill up without startling him. He sat up and stretched, wincing at the pain in his arm. "Why are you wakin' me up?" he yawned.

"You are about to experience something extraordinary."

Bill thought for a moment, still not fully awake. "Really. You mean something else?"

Russell chuckled softly at this. "Yes, something you have never experienced and only a few humans in the past have felt. I had mentioned this to you earlier."

"Can I get me some breakfast first?"

"There's no time, and besides, I would prefer you didn't anyway."

"Why's that?"

"Well, some people have an adverse reaction to what's about to happen, and it isn't very pleasant. In fact it can be downright dangerous. I'll explain after you use the bathroom and wake up a bit."

Bill sighed. He stood and shuffled to the toilet to relieve himself. After he flushed, he noticed the water didn't fill the bowl. He wiggled the handle, but nothing happened. "Hey, I think my piss bowl is broken."

"It isn't. The ship is preparing for what's about to happen."

Bill had learned to be patient and wait for Russell to tell him why things happened on this vessel. He sighed again and washed his hands and face, then sat back down on his chair. "Okay, explain."

"You have reached the half-way point in your journey, and it's time to turn the ship around."

"Oh yeah, you did say something about being weightless."

"Yes. You see, you and the ship are traveling very fast right now in the direction of where the Earth was in space before the war. The Earth is passing you in our three dimensions even as we speak, only from your point of view in the fourth dimension it is traveling backward in space and time. It will continue to do so as long as you are traveling faster than the speed of light in this direction. It is time for the ship to stop accelerating and start decelerating at the same rate. So we have to turn the ship around and project the gravity well back the way you came."

Bill thought again. "Okay, I think I understand. So this 'extraordinary experience' I'm supposed to have is weightlessness."

"Yes. It should be very thrilling."

Bill thought about that for a moment. "So you mean…"

"Yes. You are going to go from being very heavy as you accelerate—to weighing nothing in an instant when you coast."

"Oh." Bill looked around the cabin of the ship. "So what do I do?"

"Well, some people have a strong reaction to this by becoming very nauseated. It is called 'motion sickness.' So I need you to take a bag out of this compartment." He sent a mental image of where it was. "And keep it with you at all times during the transfer."

"Wait, nause…what is that?"

"It means you might throw up. If you do so in a weightless environment, it will go all over the cabin instead of falling to your feet."

Bill looked around at the electronics and shiny clean surfaces he had worked to maintain. "Oh, okay. I can see where that might be bad." He got up from his chair, wincing again at the pain in his arm and shoulder, and shuffled over to the compartment. As he was opening the drawer, the ship's computer voiced a warning.

"Engine power-down in one minute."

Bill looked around again. "Man, you don't give me much time to prepare."

Russell chuckled again. "Other than getting the bag, there's nothing for you to do but enjoy the ride. Everything else is taken care of by the ship's computer."

At thirty seconds the computer began counting down. Bill said, "Should I be strapped in or something?"

"If you like, but you might enjoy the experience more if you are not."

Bill had moved back to his chair and was standing next to it when the computer reached zero. Instantly the quiet hum of the engines began to grow even quieter, and Bill felt himself get lighter. Within a couple of seconds he felt the pressure of the floor on his feet diminish to nothing as his stomach seemed to come up into his chest. He grabbed onto the back of his seat and said, "Oh shit!" He had let go of the bag to grab the seat with both hands, and now it floated in front of his face, spinning slowly.

The computer voiced, "Engine stop complete. Beginning pitch maneuver." In the almost complete quiet, Bill heard a new noise. A soft whooshing sound filled the cabin for about three seconds as it began to slowly rotate around him. Bill let go of the seat and grabbed for the spinning bag as violent nausea gripped him. The spinning room made it so much worse. He closed his eyes, clutching the bag to his chest with one hand and holding onto the chair with the other. The chair was turning slowly in his hand, and that was too much. He was almost too late as he let go of the chair and opened the bag, launching his last meal into it. Curled into a ball with his eyes closed, he floated around the cabin while bumping into walls and throwing up.

Finally he was dry-heaving, and then his body mercifully stopped trying. He tried to spit into the bag to get the awful taste out of his mouth, but this caused some of the considerable contents to blow back into his face. He gagged again and closed the bag. When he opened his eyes, he tried to orient himself in the cabin to find something with which to clean himself up. He was near the ceiling looking at his chair through a series of vomit droplets that varied in size. Luckily there were relatively few to contend with.

The ship's computer announced, "Pitch maneuver nearing completion. Engine start in thirty seconds." There was another whooshing sound like the first and that disorienting feeling of the ship rotating around him again, seemingly in the other direction. He was hanging onto a cable near the ceiling when the countdown ended and the engines started up again with their soft hum.

"William, I know you are miserable right now, but you must let go of the cable." Bill felt himself begin to be tugged toward the floor, and his first reaction was to hold on tighter. "*Bill, let go!*" The voice was so loud, he let go of the cable and clamped his hands to his head, one of them still holding the bag tightly closed with its unpleasant contents. The engines had come on slowly, and his landing on the floor of the cabin was gentle as the droplets fell around him like a slow-motion, yellowish rain. He sat on the floor with his back against the chair, eyes closed, and tried not to move as he steadily got heavier. He had never felt that sick so suddenly in his life.

After a while he opened his eyes and looked around. He managed to crawl to the garbage chute and throw the bag in. He grabbed a towel to clean his face and hands and then threw it into the garbage. He rinsed out his mouth in the sink, and when he spit out the water, he started dry-heaving again, but not as long this time. He got another towel and went into the cabin, where he cleaned up his seat and the floor as best he could. After disposing of the second towel, he sat back in his chair and closed his eyes again. "Russell," he croaked.

"Yes, William."

"The next time you have one of those 'extraordinary experiences' for me...don't."

Chapter 47

Ramey crept to the old woman's house in the meager light of a half moon. At least she didn't have any pesky dogs. There were a couple of cats, but they just hissed and ran under the house. He didn't worry about making too much noise because the old lady probably couldn't hear a tornado ripping her house apart. He went around to the back, ducking below the side windows just in case. He tried the back door, and surprisingly, it was unlocked—not very smart with all the bad people around these days. *Poor old woman was likely to get hurt if she didn't take precautions*, he thought and smiled to himself.

He pulled the door open and then heard a noise from inside that sounded like a stack of empty cans falling over. He looked at the inside of the door in the feeble light and saw a string attached to the knob. It led off into the darkness of what appeared to be the kitchen.

Then he heard the old woman's voice. "Mayday, mayday, I have an intruder!" she screamed from her bedroom.

Then he heard another female voice, this time coming from the tinny speaker of a radio. "Copy Mrs. Dogen, tank dispatched."

"Whoever you are, I have a gun! And that tank will be here in less time than you think!" Mrs. Dogen yelled with toothless sincerity.

Damn-it! Before Ramey turned to run, he noticed a small metal box on the counter near the door. He grabbed it and took off through the garden into the early morning darkness, angrily trampling as many vegetables as he could along the way.

* * *

After what he knew must have been miles of running, the sun was making the eastern horizon glow. He found a copse of trees with a small dirty stream flowing through it. He tossed the tin box to the muddy bank and fell face-first, drinking the murky water in great swallows. It tasted crappy and wonderful at the same time. He stopped periodically to gulp in air and then resumed drinking until he felt like he couldn't hold any more water.

He sat up on the bank and felt for his canteen so he could re-fill it but then remembered he had stowed his gear before going up to that old bitch's house. He'd have to go back for it later when things cooled off. He looked around and found the tin box lying in the mud. Leaning over, he retrieved it and wiped off some of the mud. At least he'd find out what those bastards were giving her that was so important. He pried off the lid and looked inside. Candy. That old bitch grew a garden, probably working her ass off at it, and for what? Small pieces of taffy wrapped in paper. Son of a bitch. He almost threw the tin into the creek in frustration but then stopped. He hadn't had candy in a very long time, and it did smell pretty tempting.

Oh well, he thought as he grabbed the first piece, *at least this little adventure wasn't a total loss.*

Chapter 48

Bill was pacing around his seat in the Kronos. His trip was finally coming to an end, and he was suffering from cabin fever, anxious to get outside at last.

He had been awake when the ship moved from beyond light speed a while back, and he had again felt the strange sideways motion, this time leaving the fourth dimension. At least he had his eyes closed, and the flash didn't blind him. The vivid dreams had stopped, but the pain had spread from his arm and shoulder to his back. It wasn't always there but when it came back it would hit him without warning, and quite severely at times. The herbal teas had helped at first, but their effects were becoming weaker. He was going to need something stronger soon or he wouldn't be able to sleep. Thankfully it wasn't bothering him at the moment—he would have to use his arms and back soon enough.

He was now dressed in blue jeans and a flannel shirt with a denim jacket. He was also wearing cowboy boots that were quite comfortable. He had tried these on while preparing for the trip. Russell had instructed him that these clothes would allow him to blend in with the local population, no matter how out-of-place he felt wearing them. He stopped pacing and looked out a porthole near the floor again. He could see the crescent of the Moon beyond the approaching Earth. The Kronos was coming in on the dark side of the planet, and the Sun was no longer in view.

"Okay, Russell, one more time."

"Of course, William. You are approaching over the Gulf of Mexico to touch down about a mile off the coast of Galveston Island. As the Kronos nears the water, the door will open and it will stop. You are to reach outside and press the button on the left side of the door, which will deploy the inflatable raft attached with a rope. You must then place these pre-packed items in the raft." He sent mental images of a large backpack and an old beat up suitcase and where they were stowed. "In addition, you are to retrieve these three objects and place them in the backpack." He sent a mental image of three extraordinary-looking rocks, which were stored in a compartment over his chair. "Then you are to detach the raft and row to the shore, which will be lit up and easy to find. Once there, I will give you further instructions. Do you understand?"

"Yeah, I think so, but what will happen to the ship?"

"It will sink to the bottom of the gulf."

"What? You mean I can't use it for—"

"For what, William? It has served its purpose and must not be found by the authorities before you complete the mission. It would cause too much controversy and might even jeopardize the operation. Besides, the seawater is perfect for rendering the nuclear fuel undetectable. Everything you need is in the backpack and the case, including a considerable amount of cash."

"You mean like in those movies?"

"Yes. Remember how important it was to have money? It will get you where you need to be and allow you to purchase food and other accommodations along the way. Don't worry, if you follow my instructions, you won't run out."

Bill looked out the porthole again and could no longer see the bright line of the Earth off to one side. Instead he could see the darkness below that was punctuated with areas of faint light. It had patterns and lines in it, making the view quite different than the one he had left seemingly a lifetime ago. "What is that?"

"Those are cities. They are full of people leading their lives, not knowing what is to come in a few months. The war hasn't happened yet, and civilization is thriving. There are roadways connecting the cities where thousands of automobiles travel each day. Airplanes fly through the air and ships travel the oceans. There are governments and countries, and people don't have to fend for themselves just to survive. It is quite a different world than the one you left, William."

The ship began to be buffeted by the air as it entered the atmosphere and went subsonic, already slowed enough to prevent frictional heating but moving quickly enough to rock gently with the turbulence. Bill hardly noticed. "It sounds…complicated."

Russell chuckled at this. "It can be. But don't worry, I'll be here to help you

151

get through it. Now, you are getting closer to your destination, so the computer will cut the lights soon. We don't want anyone to see your approach, especially the military. They won't be able to see you on their sensors because of a special coating on the ship."

The lights turned off and the computer voiced, "Covert mode activated."

The city lights seemed brighter now, and there was a large lit-up area off to one side of the porthole. "Is that…"

"Yes, that is Houston, where I am now, but in the past. The smaller, elongated city below you is Galveston."

Bill could see a string of lights between the two areas that seemed to be moving slowly and guessed these were automobiles. He watched as the two areas slid off to one side of the porthole, and the darkness below him filled his view. The computer announced, "Approaching destination, preparing ship for abandonment." As the ride smoothed out, a series of motors whirred, and the door opened with a loud hiss. Bill could feel the cool air enter the cabin and smelled the salt of the ocean.

"The weather seems to be cooperating with us," Russell said, "the waves appear to be quite smooth."

"That's good. I don't want to have to swim a mile with this shoulder."

The computer announced, "Ship stop in thirty seconds." Bill felt the ship slowing down as he felt even heavier for a moment. As the countdown continued, however, he felt himself getting lighter as his perceived gravity shifted to that of the Earth. He could hear the sounds of the water now, with occasional small waves cresting in the calm breeze. The ship stopped about two feet from the tops of these waves and hovered in the air. A dim light came on somewhere outside near the bottom of the ship, and Bill saw a strange sight. He stood in the doorway and looked out at a wall-like mound of water about five feet high that created a ring around the ship. It started about fifteen feet from the ramp and crested about twenty feet away. The mound was motionless with small waves crisscrossing it, but little tendrils of water were being pulled off the top and they disappeared upward and out of sight.

"What the hell?"

"That is the effect of the gravity well, and it is something you will have to contend with after leaving the ship. The gravity shield has been extended some.

It is time to deploy the raft."

Bill stepped down onto the first step of the door and looked for the button. It was there, as promised, and he pressed it. A compartment opened on the bottom of the ship and another loud hiss filled the air as the raft splashed into the water and began to inflate. Bill went back into the Kronos and found the items he needed to take with him. Everything felt so *light*. He climbed up and stood on the seat to retrieve the stones out of their special compartment. These were quite heavy, in spite of everything else seeming so light. They were also very warm, as if they were generating their own heat. "What are these?" he asked, hefting them in his hands. They were white with multi-colored sparkles in the dim light and were quite beautiful.

"Those I will explain later, but you must handle them carefully. They are very important to your mission. Place then in the inner pocket of the backpack, where they will be protected."

Bill did so, and when he returned to the door, the raft was full and floating peacefully below the ship. He stepped down again and carefully placed the backpack and suitcase into the small craft. Then he paused and looked around the interior of the ship, knowing he would never again see his home of the last two months. The dim lights of the computer reflected off the shiny metal surfaces and the soft leather of his chair. It seemed like such a waste to let all this sink to the bottom of the ocean. After a last lingering look, he reached for the rope attached to the side of the ship and pulled the raft below the ramp. The oval vessel was about six feet long and three feet wide with a seat toward one end. He stepped in and sat down. Feeling around the small boat, he found a short wooden oar tucked under one side.

"William, you need to untie the raft. Quickly now." Bill complied. "Good. Now row toward the lights. As hard as you can."

"I can't see the lights. The water is in the way."

"Of course." Russell sent him a mental image that gave him a perspective from above himself, showing that the direction he was facing was toward the lights but slightly to the right. He now knew which direction to row and did so. When he reached the ring of water, he found it was easy to row up the side because the gravity well was pulling him up as he moved. It was actually more difficult to row down the other side for the same reason. He had to keep

153

switching sides with his rowing so the raft wouldn't spin in one place, and his right shoulder was starting to feel like it had ground-up glass in the joint. After what seemed like an eternity, but was actually less than two minutes, he had escaped the ship's artificial gravity well.

Russell said, "William, stop and rest for a moment. You need to see this."

"What?" Before Russell could answer, Bill heard a soft splash behind him. He turned the raft, and in the faint glow from shore he saw that the Kronos was now in the water and sinking. The ring-mound of water had disappeared. He heard popping and saw flashes of light as the water entered the cabin and shorted out the electronics. After a moment, the open door was below the surface and emitting fountains of bubbles, which made different, short-lived mounds on the surface. In seconds, the ship had disappeared, and the bubbles were slowing. Bill suddenly felt that his way back was completely cut off now. Moments earlier, he wanted nothing more than to get out of the ship. Now he longed to be back aboard. Even though he had suspected all along that he could never go back, it was a cold harsh reality now. He thought of David and Pete from his village. He thought of his wife and daughters and the memories that had been hidden from him. He thought of the road ahead of him, full of uncertainties and confusion. Without another word, he turned the raft and began to row once more toward the shore.

Chapter 49

Bill woke to a sound he hadn't heard since his youth. Seagulls were fighting over something he couldn't yet see on the other side of a dune. Although by the sound of it, whatever they were fighting over was the funniest thing in the world, their loud calls sounding like maniacal laughter. He remembered hearing and seeing the large gray and white birds when his mother took him to the beach as a youth, along with a group of well-armed men. He couldn't recall the reason for the trip, but he never forgot the sight and sounds of the adventure.

It was the twilight before dawn, and there was just enough illumination from the multi-colored sky for Bill to see his surroundings. Following Russell's directions, he had brought the raft ashore, deflated it with a small knife from the backpack, and carried it and the contents inland to a dark, remote area in the sand dunes. There he dug a hole and buried the raft. He had found it difficult to walk at first because he was not used to feeling so light. It seemed with every step he took he would launch into the air. Russell had told him it would do no good to try to travel at that hour, so he found a grassy area and relaxed, using the backpack as a pillow and listening to the quiet waves washing ashore in the distance as he quickly drifted off to sleep.

Now he could see that he was in a depression surrounded by dunes that were dotted with clumps of tall grass. There were dying vines with triangular-shaped leaves covering some of the area except for the patch where he now sat, which was covered with a shorter grass. The backpack and case were exactly as he had left them. He stood and dusted the loose sand off his clothes before climbing to the top of the nearest dune.

He had a superior view of the area from here. Toward the ocean was the beachfront, where a man was waving a long pole back and forth. Bill watched as the man finally stopped and pointed the pole out to sea. A moment later there was a splash quite a way out, and the man fiddled with something on the bottom of the pole before shoving it into some kind of holder in the sand. Seemingly satisfied with his work, the man sat down and watched the pole.

"That's called fishing." Russell's voice startled Bill, who had been watching the man intently. "It's a method of catching fish to eat."

"I don't understand."

"That splash you saw was bait on a sharp metal hook. When the fish eats the bait, the hook catches the fish in the mouth. It is attached to a long thin string, which is attached to the pole. You're just too far away to see the string, but it's there."

"Oh. Why doesn't he just trap the fish?"

"Well, he could, but this way is more enjoyable. He's not fishing because he needs the food, he's doing it because he wants to relax. One of the benefits of living in a civilized age is something called spare time. It comes from not having to struggle for survival all the time."

"Oh yeah. I remember from watching those movies."

"Exactly. You've seen children playing while the grownups work. Well this is play for the adults."

"Seems kind of wasteful. Shouldn't he be doing some kind of work?"

"Oh, I'm sure he does. But this is his spare time."

Bill shook his head. "This place is going to take some getting used to."

Russell chuckled. "Don't worry, you won't be here that long if everything goes well. Are you hungry?"

"Yeah. Where do I get food?"

"Look to your left."

Bill did and realized he had been so busy watching the fisherman he hadn't noticed that he was near a city. Up the beach were shops that crowded the waterfront, and behind them were more and larger buildings. In the growing light, he could see movement outside them. A few cars were making their way down the streets with their headlights on. People were walking around the structures and on the beach, and some of them were accompanied by small animals he guessed to be dogs. In some of the buildings, the windows were lit up from inside—even the tall ones. And though he had seen the movies, he had never seen any of these things before with his own eyes. As strangely familiar as all this was, it still made the place seem somehow hostile and alien to him.

"William, I need you to listen to me carefully. I will guide you through this place and help you as much as possible, but you must never talk to me unless we are alone. Others cannot hear my voice, and it would look like you were talking to yourself. That sort of behavior is frowned upon in society because it makes you look insane. Might even get you in trouble with the authorities, which is something we need to avoid at all costs. Do you understand?"

"Got it. You'll tell me what to say, right?"

"Yes. Don't worry, you'll do fine."

"And the mission?"

"Right now your mission is to get you something to eat. Grab your packs and walk toward those buildings."

Chapter 50

Ramey checked the fish trap for the third time—still nothing. He sat down under a bald cypress tree on the bank of the creek and listened to his stomach rumble. To make matters worse, the sky began to echo his tummy, and fat drops of rain were beginning to fall. He watched them splash into the water and saw fish surfacing and snapping at them. Stupid creek seemed to be mocking him with its bounty of fish, which were too stupid to go into his stupid fish trap. He had baited it with a large grasshopper—a large stupid grasshopper.

As he sat watching the sparse rain, he heard another noise. It was the unmistakable whirring sound of one of those tanks his brother owned. There were more and more of these things around now, and he deduced that they were still building them—even though, or probably because, his army had destroyed a good number of them. He crawled into some nearby bushes at the bank's rim and waited. To his surprise, the tank was coming right toward him. It stopped a few feet before going over the embankment, right next to his bushes, and shut down its engine. The slowly falling rain had stopped, and now only the gurgling creek could be heard. Nothing happened for a minute, and then the door opened on the side.

He heard one of the occupants say, "Just give me a minute. And radio in to get that toilet fixed when we get back." He heard a muffled reply as one of the men walked down the steps and around the front of the tank, passing just inches from where he was hiding. The man was in the usual white jumpsuit these idiots always wore, and he was making his way down the bank to the creek. There he unfastened the jumpsuit and began to pee in the creek.

Ramey was swift and silent in his attack. He pulled the knife from the scabbard on his waist and quietly approached the pissing man. He placed his left hand over the man's mouth and pulled him against his body while he sliced the man's throat with the knife. Then he gently laid the man down on his back and waited until he was perfectly still, open eyes staring up into the cloudy sky. Then he scrambled back to his hiding place to wait.

After a few minutes, the other occupant stuck his head outside the tank door and called, "Tim!" When he heard no reply, he yelled, "Tim, don't make me break protocol and come out there. I don't want to have to look at your dingus leaking all over the ground!" Still no reply. Then he mumbled, "Son of a bitch," as he disappeared back into the tank. In a few moments he emerged wearing a gun-belt with a large-caliber pistol. He started down the bank and froze when he saw his partner's bloody body. He had begun to pull out the firearm when he felt the knife enter his own neck and felt blood flowing over his chest. The pistol fell from his fingers, and he reached for his throat, just as the world went black for him.

Ramey removed the man's gun-belt and wiped the blood off in the grass before putting it on himself. He picked up the pistol and cleaned off the mud. It was a .44 magnum and seemed to be in good shape. Then he quietly walked up to the tank and peered inside while pointing the .44 where he looked. He was alone. He re-holstered the gun and entered the tank, rummaging around for something to eat. He found manuals and tools, but nothing looked promising. Then he spotted the lunchbox. It was wedged under one of the seats, and he grabbed for it desperately. He opened it and was greeted with the heavenly smells of bacon and cornbread. After devouring the contents greedily, he found the second lunchbox and enjoyed the wonders of ham-beans and rice with a couple of boiled eggs on the side. Damn, his brother had everything good. He washed it all down with some half-warm herbal tea as he looked around the tank.

The controls seemed pretty simple: a steering wheel, a shift knob marked "F" and "R," two pedals on the floor, and screens to see where you were going—almost like driving a car. All he had to do was learn how to work the radio and try to mimic the younger voices he had heard earlier. He thought he could do okay. He had found a manual when he was looking for food called "Radio Instructions & Protocols," and now he sat down to skim through it. He had also found one called "Weapons Systems," and that was going to be next. *Yes,* he thought, *this is going to work out just fine!*

Chapter 51

Bill chewed his first bite of pancakes and closed his eyes. They were covered in melted butter and soaked with hot maple syrup. He had never tasted anything so good in his life. So good in fact, he felt overwhelmed in anticipation of taking the next bite. Nothing else in the world mattered right now.

Russell had guided him to a diner near the beach and instructed him how to conduct himself so as not to draw attention. By just about all appearances, he was a normal customer who had ordered breakfast a thousand times before. The only thing that set him apart now was the almost comical look of ecstasy on his face as he ate. His waitress was a rather large woman with dark curly hair, wearing a pink dress with a white apron. He was sitting at the counter, and she stopped in front of him while holding a pot of coffee. Her nametag said she was called Bess.

She looked at him and smiled. "Honey, I know they're good, but you look like you're in heaven."

"Ma'am, this is the best stuff I've ever eaten in my life," Bill said around a mouthful of pancakes.

"Really?" Her smile faltered a little. "Where you from?"

Bill thought quickly and then said dismissively, "A real small town. Long way from here."

Bess said, "Well, Chuck will be glad to hear that you like his hot cakes, and welcome to Galveston!" Then she ambled off to fill coffee cups.

Russell said amiably, "Try not to talk with food in your mouth. It's considered impolite." Bill nodded once. "I know you're thinking there are too many rules to remember." Bill nodded again and took another bite. Russell chuckled. "Don't worry, I'll help you. But right now I envy you. Those do look delicious."

Bill finished the stack of pancakes and stood up to leave.

Bess saw this and asked, "You need your check?"

Russell quickly explained that he needed to pay for his food here and told him to take one dollar out of his pocket. He had instructed Bill earlier to take some of the money out of the backpack and had him look at it carefully. Bill had quickly learned about ones, fives, tens, and twenties. He laid the money on the counter and said, "Thank you, ma'am. It was really good."

"Oh, honey, that's the breakfast special. It's only seventy-five cents. Let me get your change."

Under Russell's instruction Bill said, "No ma'am, it was *real* good," and smiled broadly.

"Well, thank you, hon!" Bess returned his smile.

Bill picked up his belongings and walked out of the diner into the morning sunshine. The air was cool and humid with a slight breeze blowing and had a salty tinge. Russell was telling him which direction to walk, and as he did so, Bill looked around with interest. He could make sense of some things, like cars and gas stations, but other things baffled him. Some of the women, for example, had very tall hairstyles while others did not. Some people had white, smoldering, foul-smelling sticks in their mouths. He vaguely remembered his mother talking about this but couldn't remember what they were called. Cigarettes, Russell informed him. And the clothes they wore—very strange.

With his backpack and case, which he had kept next to him in the diner, he looked like a drifter. Most people avoided him, if they noticed him at all. Russell had him traveling in a northeastern pattern, zigzagging through greater Galveston toward some destination unknown to Bill. He passed shops, industrial buildings, and residential areas—all of which were fascinating to him.

Finally he arrived at a long building, behind which were parked several large vehicles with lots of windows. They were sitting on steel tracks that he had come across several times in his past. He remembered they were called "train tracks," but he didn't know what they were for. "This is a train depot, William. It is where you will procure transportation for your next leg of the mission."

Bill looked around and saw that he was alone for the time being. He said softly, "Transportation? Where am I going?"

"You'll see. Go inside and look for a window marked 'Tickets.'" Bill did, and when he approached it, Russell told him what to say.

The man behind the window said, "That's the nine-fifteen train with a stop and changeover in Houston. It'll be eighteen dollars." Bill gave him a twenty and took the change. He started to turn away, but the man said, "Here, you might need this," and handed him the ticket. Bill took it and stood there staring at it. Russell had to tell him to go sit down and stop staring at the ticket. Bill sat on a bench but couldn't help looking at the ticket some more. It was a card, slightly smaller than the money, but with words, letters, and numbers he didn't understand.

"What am I supposed to do with this?" he mumbled.

"You give it to the porter and he'll punch it for you. Then you get on board and just ride the train."

"What's a porter?"

"He'll be waiting outside next to the train, wearing a uniform and loading luggage. Since you're traveling light you can carry your bags on board with you."

"Oh, okay. Sounds simple enough." He looked around the train station and saw a few other people also waiting but at enough distance that he wouldn't be overheard. "Tell me something, Russell. How do you manage to be with me all the time? Don't you have a village to run?"

"Well, William, I'm actually not with you all the time. Remember how I said I could travel to the past in this form and visit any moment I wanted?"

"Yes."

"All right, here's what I do. I can leave you at any time and go take a nap or eat or visit or even see to an activity that takes days. Then all I have to do is come right back to a moment after I left you, and it seems to you that I never left at all. It's because you're becoming part of the past now. Do you understand?"

"Oh, I get it. I guess."

At that moment, an announcement came over the PA system that reminded Bill of Russell talking in his head, only this time everyone looked up. The message said his train would begin boarding in fifteen minutes.

"Well," Bill said quietly, "I'm going to go visit the...uh, what was it...the restroom before I leave. You don't have to come along, if you don't want to."

"All right. I think I'll go to bed. Talk to you in a few minutes."

162

Chapter 52

The tank drove like a dream. Smooth ride, powerful motor, and it was quiet. The evening after Ramey had "acquired" the vehicle, he had driven up on a small herd of deer and slaughtered some of them with the laser weapon before they could bound away. He had stopped and begun roasting a deer leg over a fire when the radio crackled to life. "Star Eight this is Star One. Respond."

He heard the radio through the open door of the tank from where he was sitting by the fire. He had studied the maps and routes carefully and had taken a route of his own, far from their prying eyes. Now he got up and went into the tank. Thinking for a moment how the men had sounded, he tried his best to imitate the last one he had heard. "This is Star Eight. Go."

"Star Eight, where are you? Your report time was half an hour ago."

"Have some mechanical problems, should be fixed within the hour."

"Why didn't you report in, James?"

So that was the second guy's name. "Sorry, guess we forgot."

After a few moments' pause, "There is no excuse for this behavior and it will be reported."

"Yeah, I know."

Another pause. "Where are you, exactly? And why isn't your transponder working?"

He consulted a map. "Uh…sector 7, C-5, by the ravine. And our transponder is part of the problem." He was nowhere near there, and he had smashed the transponder as soon as he found it with help from the manual.

"We'll send a mechanic out."

"Well, okay, but I think we can fix it."

"Just sit tight. Star One out."

"Star Eight out."

That should keep them busy for a while. He went back to his deer leg and turned it again. It was starting to get a little burned on one side, but it smelled wonderful. He thought about the mechanic going out to the place where he had said he was and not finding him there. He would look and look, and then the radio calls would start. Ramey wasn't going to answer, and they would have to start looking in the heavily forested area near the ravine. Ol' James would have no reason to lie, so he must be there somewhere. Then the search would be called off until daylight, and they would look again…but nothing would be there. Oh, the wives or friends of those poor bastards Tim and James would have to be notified, and there would be tears and worry. That made him smile.

He sliced off a small piece of deer leg and put the hot meat gingerly in his mouth. It had a bit of a wild, gamey flavor, but it was juicy and tender. He swallowed it hungrily and cut off more. It took him the better part an hour and a half to get full, but most of the leg was gone when the radio came to life again.

"Star Eight this is Star Ten…." He sat and listened, amused. "Star Eight this is Star Ten, how do you read?" After a few moments, "Star One this is Star Ten."

"Go ahead Star Ten."

"We find no sign of Star Eight at the given coordinates. Not on radar, visual, or thermal. And they're not answering their radio."

After a few moments, "Star Ten stand by."

"Star Ten, standing by."

Oh, this was going to be fun. Ramey found he could fit one more bite of venison in and cut it off the bone.

"Star Ten, this is Star One. Make a careful search of the area, but do not, repeat, do not enter the woods or the ravine. Search party is being dispatched and should arrive within the hour."

"Copy Star One. Beginning search, Star Ten out."

Perfect. These fish were swimming into his trap much easier than the real ones. The more they sent, the better. Now all he had to do was wait, listen to the radio, and count.

Chapter 53

Bill sat on the train for what seemed like an eternity before it finally began moving. He had stowed his bags in an overhead bin and was sitting by a large window that looked out on the right side of the train into the depot yard. The aisle seat next to him was empty. As he looked out the window, he saw several tracks parallel to the one his train was sitting on, with cars and engines here and there waiting to be used. Russell had been anticipating most of his questions and was explaining much of what he was looking at for him. Finally the train began to move, and Bill couldn't help but feel a little thrill at traveling again, although this was much slower than he had become accustomed to. There were about ten other people in the car, and some of them were talking animatedly, obviously thrilled to be traveling as well.

The train pulled out of the depot and along an unattractive beach where pipes and dirty-looking fenced-off areas dominated the view. Abruptly, the train took a right turn, and he was on a long bridge over dull-brown water. Russell informed him, "This is the bridge that connects the island to the mainland. There is a new bridge for motor traffic on the other side of the train." Bill looked out the left windows and saw the bridge with occasional cars passing in both directions.

"Isn't that something?" An older gentleman was sitting in the seat just across the aisle, next to what appeared to be his daughter, who was sitting by the window. From what he could tell, she was a nice-looking woman. They were both staring out at the bridge as well. "I can remember a few years ago when it was an older bridge like this one here. Rough as all get-out." He turned to Bill. "You remember that, young man?"

Bill thought for a moment and then said, "No. I'm new to the area."

At hearing that, the woman turned to look at Bill. He had only seen her from the side, but when she looked at him, he was struck by her intense beauty. She had dark, straight, shoulder-length hair and alabaster skin with full crimson lips. Her almond-shaped eyes were large and almost black. When she saw the look on his face, she couldn't help but smile. With that smile, her eyes disappeared into long eyelashes, making her almost too beautiful to bear.

Russell said, "William stop staring, you're making a scene."

Bill tore his eyes away and looked out his own window. The old man had been watching this with some amusement. He laughed softly and said, "Don't worry son, she gets that a lot. This is Katy, my daughter, and I'm Harland. We're on our way up to Waco to visit my son."

Bill turned to them, smiled, and said, "Pleased to meet you. My name is Bill." He said this to Harland but couldn't help glancing at Katy again. Once again his eyes stopped at her smiling face. And once again he had to tear them away.

When she spoke, her voice was smooth, like that of an exotic song-bird. "Now, stop it daddy. You're making him nervous," she said. Bill could hear in her voice that she knew she was the one doing that. She had a soft southern accent that reminded Bill of a cool drink of clear water on a hot day.

Russell sensed what was going on and said, "William there's something I must warn you about. You mustn't interact with anyone here any more than you absolutely have to. It could be dangerous." Bill didn't respond but kept staring out his window. He knew if he looked back at her he would just stare again. Russell continued. "Your presence here is already changing the past as we know it. If you interact with the wrong person, you could set off a chain of events that affects one or both of our futures, and this might cause you never to be sent back in time. If that happens it could create a paradox."

Bill stood up and said to the old man and his daughter, "Excuse me," as he made his way to the back of the train car where Russell had earlier told him the restroom was. He bumped his right shoulder as he went through the door, and a searing pain caused him to inhale sharply and wince. He locked the door, then sat on the toilet fully clothed, rubbing the sore area. "Okay, what the hell is a paradox?" he asked softly.

"A paradox is just what I said. You can prevent your own trip through time. This must not be done before the mission is complete."

"You know my arm is killing me, and now you're giving me a headache, too. What would happen if I did this 'paradox' thing?"

"Well, actually, that is your mission, to create a paradox. But not yet and not this way."

"Seriously. A big headache."

"Do you remember those stones I had you retrieve from the Kronos, just before it sank?"

"Yeah, they're in the backpack. I was gonna ask you about those."

"Well, they're made of a special mineral found in the Earth. It was considerably difficult to come by, but we found it near some mines in western Arkansas…or what used to be called Arkansas. It is considered a semi-precious gemstone called raw opal, but my friends from across the galaxy taught me what it can do under the right conditions. That compartment you retrieved it from was exposed to certain kinds of radiation while you were traveling through space. As a result, those stones absorbed that radiation and are now time stabilizers."

Bill was listening intently. "Okay, what do they do?"

"You see, as the Earth travels through space, it leaves an imprint on the fabric of space behind it. It is very faint and not detectable by any means of current technology. This imprint is a recording of radiation emitted from the Earth. People and their thoughts emit this radiation, much like what you're receiving from me now. This is how I find you so easily, no matter where you are."

"Okay."

"Well, that special radiation is what was collected and recorded by the stones as you traveled along the path of the Earth at both hyper- and sub-light speeds. Now, if something significant happens on Earth, it causes a lot of people to put attention on it. Great wars for example, especially the last one. All that attention emits a similar radiation pattern, which is now stored in the stones. They are following along with you and the Earth as it replays the information right now, slowly releasing that radiation. If something significantly different were to happen than what is stored in the stones, causing a lot of people to emit a different pattern of radiation, it would cause a disruption of the energy stored in the stones and it will be released all at once. This has the effect of stabilizing the difference in history…within a limited distance because the stones are small. You're going to use them to change history. That's the mission, remember? To prevent the great war."

"I think I see now. Because if I changed history to prevent the war, then I would never have come back in time to change history and prevent the war, right?"

"Exactly. Hence the paradox. You're going to make a change, and the stones will stabilize it and make it...*stick*."

Bill thought it over, then something occurred to him. "Wait a minute. You can talk to other people in this time, right?"

"Yes, I could..."

"Why didn't you just grab some person from this time and make him do all this? I mean, sure would've saved you a lot of trouble. You know, building the ship and all."

"I'm afraid it would have caused the same problem, another paradox. If I had done that and prevented the war that way, then I wouldn't have been able to do that, do you see? It took someone traveling back in time and recording the radiation history with the stones to make the change stable. Trust me William, I have thought of any number of scenarios and this mission is the only way."

Bill considered this for a while. "Yeah, I can see that you've thought about this a lot. So, when I change history what happens to me?"

"You'll have to stay far enough away from the stones so you don't get stuck there in the past. It would continue to create a paradox if you did."

Bill thought a bit more, and felt another twinge of pain in his shoulder as he did. "Yeah, I guess sticking around here would be a bad idea anyway."

Chapter 54

"Star Ten, this is Star One. Report."

"Star Ten here. Star Seven just arrived with the search gear. We are about to begin our search of the woods and the ravine. If they're out here, we'll find them."

"Copy. We need updates every half hour. Be careful out there, Hank."

"Copy. Star Ten out."

Now, Ramey thought. *Now it's time to pay that city of theirs a little visit.* He consulted the map again. There was a main, well-traveled road between the city and the search area. He followed it on the paper with one hairy-knuckled finger. He was going to have to avoid this road and approach from a different angle if he didn't want to be seen.

If his stupid brother weren't out there, he could leave his body and check the area for sure. But he *was* out there. Ramey wondered why he hadn't sensed his brother leaving his body to join the search. Something was distracting him— something more important than watching over his beloved idiots. He didn't know what it was, but it bothered him. It made his need to get into that city and end his brother's wretched life all the more urgent. Whatever his brother was doing, Ramey was going to ruin his plans. You could bet on that.

He started the tank and headed for an area about five miles from the city. There he could turn toward the city and avoid being noticed by anyone until he was almost at the gate. As he drove along, he listened to the radio chatter about the search. Poor guys weren't having any luck. He began humming a tuneless song and thinking about killing all those people in their comfortable little city. Maybe he'd leave a few women alive…you know, for entertainment purposes. He'd just have to see.

Ramey had intended to take the city with his army, but thanks to his idiot brother, those plans had changed. It was not going to be so easy to take the whole city by himself, but he figured he could manage. First order of business would be to find his brother and kill him. Then the rest of the fools could be slaughtered or captured, depending on his whim. With his brother gone, he could await the return of the tanks and destroy them one by one—flipping them, crushing them, or whatever he desired at the time. Then he could radio his own city to come and enjoy the bounty he had won. Oh, this was going to be such fun.

Chapter 55

The train moved quickly through the countryside, rocking gently as it passed farms, small communities, and lines of cars awaiting its passage on roads. Bill took all this in silently, knowing now it was better not to talk to anyone.

He had emerged from the train restroom and walked back to his seat, removing his items from the overhead bin without so much as a glance at the old man and his daughter. Walking to a seat nearer the back of the car, he stowed his gear again and sat down. He made a point of looking intently out the window. He saw the young woman glance his way several times with his peripheral vision but didn't return her looks. Eventually she stopped, probably guessing he was avoiding her. This made him want to look at her even more, to let her know he was very interested, but he made himself look anywhere else.

They had stopped in Houston and all gotten onto a different train, but this time Bill waited for them to board and got into a different car. He continued to avoid looking at people, so as not to invite conversations.

After boarding, he had moved to an empty seat as far from other passengers as possible. The train had departed Houston on time and was traveling north. Presently a porter came by and told everyone lunch was being served in the dining car. Some of the people in his sparsely populated car got up and moved forward on the train. Bill was getting hungry and decided to follow them.

Before he could get up, he heard, "Be careful William, dining cars are notorious for intermingling with other passengers." Bill said nothing but remained seated.

He put his left arm on the seat ahead of him and rested his forehead on it, pretending to go to sleep.

"I'm hungry. Those pancakes didn't stick with me," he whispered at the floor.

"If you can hold out for an hour or so, there's a depot stop ahead. You can buy something to eat there."

"All right, but if I starve to death your mission will fail."

Russell chuckled. "In the meantime, there are some snacks in your backpack."

"Could have told me that earlier."

Bill stood and took his backpack from the overhead bin. He sat back down, unbuckled the strap holding the top shut, and looked inside. There were several side pouches with assorted equipment and tools, and in one of the larger ones he saw some cellophane-covered items. He took one out and unwrapped it. It looked like a seed-covered stick about four inches long, but it smelled sweet. A small bite revealed an unfamiliar taste, slightly stale, but not too bad.

"That's one of our chef's grain bar recipes. Very nutritious. Try not to let anyone else see it, as it might raise some questions."

Bill looked around the train car and saw no one was looking at him. He put his head back on his arm over the seat back ahead of him and worked on eating the bar.

"When you finish your snack, I would like for you to try to take a nap. There's something I need to give you."

"Um…not sure I understand," Bill whispered.

"I need to give you some background on your mission, but it's rather a lot of information. You will perceive it as a vivid dream, but you will remember it all."

"You mean it won't be all fuzzy when I wake up? Like most dreams?"

"Exactly. This will be more like a movie you will have watched, but not quite the same. Unfortunately, there's quite a lot of information to pass, and I'm afraid if I tried to give it to you while you were awake…you might faint."

"Oh, wonderful. Another new experience," he sighed.

"Yes, but quite necessary. You did want to know your mission, did you not? This is what you have been asking me for since we met."

"Yeah, I guess so. Thought you'd just tell me the mission, though. Not…this." he gestured toward nothing, wincing at the pain in his right arm as he did so.

"As I said, all necessary. It won't be all of the mission, just some important background. As soon as you're asleep we'll get started."

172

Bill finished chewing the last bite of the bar and looked over his arm around the car. Some of the remaining passengers were dozing sitting up, and others were talking quietly or looking out at the passing countryside. He put his head back on his arm and whispered, "Sure, I'll just go right to sleep. Nothing to worry about like a new experience or anything."

"We have less than an hour before the next stop. I'll need you to sleep now."

"Sorry, you can't just tell me I'm gonna go through something like that and expect me to relax. I've had too many of your other 'experiences' and I just can't do it."

"Maybe I can give you a little push…"

"What do you me—" and Bill leaned into the corner of his seat and was out.

Chapter 56

Ramey whistled a tuneless song as he drove the tank toward the turn point. He was in quite a good mood, knowing his plan was going to come together soon. Oh, there had been some changes—drastic ones—but he was confident this new one would work. He again consulted the map and then looked at the screen in front of him. Almost all of the remaining tanks were still looking for him near the ravine, but their search would be called off soon. He didn't have much time.

The radio crackled to life. "Star One, this is Star Ten."

"Go ahead Star Ten."

"Progress report. We've sent a team to the bottom of the ravine, and they are searching for any sign. So far nothing has been sighted. Also, there are no tracks in the area. It's almost as if they were never here."

"Stand by Star Ten…transponders show you are at the correct coordinates. There was no reason for them to give a false location."

"Yes, but didn't they say they were having malfunctions? Could their navigation equipment have been off?"

There was a pause as Ramey smiled. "Star Ten, you are correct. Begin expanding your search."

"Copy, Star One, expanding search grid. Star Ten out."

"Oh, you guys are the best!" Ramey beamed. He hadn't even thought of that himself! They were giving him even more time than he had planned for. He consulted the map again and saw he was approaching a small river. "Maybe I'll just stop and have a little picnic."

He expanded the view of his forward screen and switched to infrared. The depression made by the river was visible in the distance and was approaching nicely.

"Yes, this will do just fine."

Suddenly he felt dizzy and swooned. Grabbing the seat handles, he tried to stay upright and managed to do so through tunnel vision. He stopped the tank and looked around himself wondering what was happening. Slowly the feeling passed. Deciding to do a self-assessment, he got out of the chair and sat on the floor, cross-legged. Instead of moving outside his body, he went inward, checking his vital organs: heart, liver, intestines, spleen, glands, wait…something was in his left lung. A mass that wasn't supposed to be there. He looked at it, knowing full well what it was.

Coming back to himself he said, "Well shit. Looks like I don't have as much time as I thought."

Chapter 57

Bill floated through cloudy images until he could see a clear one below him. He felt himself being pulled toward it as it grew larger. He slowed as he got closer and then dropped inside the scene. He was once again a dust mote that could look any direction he wanted to. It was somewhat like the scene where he watched his family die, but this time it was very different. He knew he had never been here before. He also knew a lot about this place that he shouldn't have known. It was in a country called the Soviet Union, a long time before the war. He was in someone's home, in the kitchen. There was a wood-burning stove, an ice box that took a block of ice to keep its contents cool, and an old wooden table with four wooden chairs. Someone was under the table. He moved closer and saw two boys, aged about eight and ten. The younger one was Andrei and the older was Vasily. They were hiding and they were very frightened. Someone else was in the house…a man whose name was Yuri: a very drunk man by the sound of it. He was speaking a foreign language that Bill had never heard before, but somehow he could understand every slurred word that spilled from the drunk's mouth. He was looking for something, and the longer he looked the angrier he was getting. "Where is my bottle of vodka?" the man said.

Under the table, Vasily turned to Andrei and whispered, "Just keep quiet," in that same language.

From the other room came "Lana! Where is my bottle?!" Bill knew this was his wife's name and that she had gone to the market earlier in the day. Realizing that he knew these things was kind of comforting, and he rolled with it. He also knew the whereabouts of this angry man's bottle of vodka. The two boys had been playing in the other room earlier and one of them had knocked it to the floor, where it had shattered. Knowing what was to come, they had cleaned it up as best they could, but had to dump the glass into the kitchen garbage pail because right then their father was stumbling up the walk. They barely had time to hide.

"Lana!" the drunk man bellowed. There was no answer. "Boys!" Both boys jumped a little but kept quiet "Where is everyone? And where is my bottle?!" The man walked unsteadily into the kitchen, looking around. He passed by the garbage pail but didn't look in. Instead he walked to the window and looked out at the darkening street. Standing there for a bit, their puzzled father then turned and took another survey of the kitchen. Still not seeing the boys, he started back toward the other room to have one more look, but this time glanced into the trash. Bill and the boys watched his every move. The drunk man continued toward the front room but then stopped in the doorway. He turned very deliberately and walked back to the garbage, staring down at it for some time. It seemed like minutes had passed before realization slowly spread across his face, which was now turning alarmingly red.

Andrei made a slight whimpering noise, and that was it. Their father turned to them and stared in fury. Vasily quietly told his younger sibling to stay put. He slowly pushed a chair from under the table and crawled out. He stood, trembling.

"It was me," he said in a desperately small voice.

The drunk man roared and charged the boy, raising his hand high above his head. Vasily winced and braced himself. When the blow fell across his face, it sounded like a gunshot. The boy flew backward hard into the table, his face burning and his left ear ringing. The drunk man was already raising his hand for more as the older brother stood up again, ready to take whatever his father was willing to give.

Bill tried to stop the man but once again could do nothing. He passed through the man's upraised hand and realized he was not part of this world. It had all happened long ago, and there was nothing he could do about it because he wasn't really there.

Under the table, Andrei was crying. Knowing better than to bring attention to himself, he sobbed quietly and witnessed his brother's beating. Bill moved down under the table to stay with the boy, knowing the poor lad was just as helpless as he was to stop this. He saw in Andrei's eyes simultaneous hatred for their father and enormous love for his brother. It had been him after all, the

177

youngest brother, who had broken the bottle of vodka. All Vasily had to do was tell the truth, and then he would be the one suffering his father's wrath. But his brother had taken the blame, and now he was being beaten to within an inch of his life. And Bill knew this wasn't the first time.

At that moment the front door opened and Lana came in with grocery bags in her arms.

"Yuri! *Stop!*"

* * *

Bill awoke to the feeling of the train slowing down. He was a bit bewildered and it took him a moment to gather his bearings. His head throbbed with every heartbeat. He looked around the car and eventually remembered where he was.

"My god!" he said quietly.

"William, are you all right?"

Bill looked around again and saw that some of the passengers were getting ready to disembark from the train, gathering bags and other belongings.

He laid his head on his left arm, once again on the seat in front of him, and whispered, "What the hell was *that*?"

"That, William, was some background. The next time we do this—"

"Next time? Really?"

"Yes. There is much more you have to learn about the mission, but I didn't want to give you too much at once."

"Oh, gee, thanks a lot. Why did I have to see that? And why does my head hurt so much?"

"Oh, you'll understand soon. You will see those two boys again. Right now, you should get off the train and get something to eat. It'll make you feel better."

"Okay. I certainly hope so."

"Tell me William, have you ever heard of a cheeseburger?"

Chapter 58

Ramey sat on the floor of the tank and thought. He had always been a superior leader, possessed with powers that would make any rival cringe with fear. His followers were always loyal—or if they weren't they would suffer the consequences. He could do so much to the world around him and make it better. At least better as he saw it. But now this. For the first time in his life, he felt powerless.

He had never faced his own mortality before, but now it had been forced upon him. He had seen many, many people die of cancer over the years. Slow, painful deaths that rarely bothered him but appeared to bother the victims quite a bit. He'd make them work until they couldn't anymore, and then he'd make them leave—even if they had to be dragged out into the wilderness to die. There were always others to replace them. But this was not supposed to happen to him. He had been certain that he was different and would somehow live forever.

He'd tried removing the cancer on some of the more important followers telekinetically, but that just made it worse. That is, if they survived the attempt at all. He knew better than to try it on himself. He could just cut himself open and take it out, but he knew he'd bleed to death if he tried. At least he had some time left.

These thoughts ran through his mind again and again, but he couldn't change it—any of it. There was no way around it—no way to fix it. He was desperate to grasp some kind of meaning for all this.

He looked around the tank, trying to comprehend why any of this mattered anymore. What was he doing out here in the wilderness, alone in one of his brother's toys? Then everything came together in a single thought…his brother. All his mixed emotions quickly turned into singular rage.

He bellowed his brother's name at the inside of the tank. If it weren't for his stinking little brother, he wouldn't have come out here into the radiation and gotten cancer. He wouldn't have been forced to eat or drink or breathe whatever it was that gave this to him. His brother. Oh, he would pay. And so would everyone he cared about.

He sprang up from the floor and sat back in the driver's seat. There would be no more stopping—no more hesitations. They were going to pay, and it would be today.

Thinking distractedly of the plan, he started the tank and began moving to the turning point at top speed.

Chapter 59

When the train pulled into the station, Bill took his belongings and stepped down onto the depot platform. Russell directed him to walk east toward one of the taller buildings. Bill was again struck by the enormity of these structures, not used to seeing them occupied and in such good repair.

He had eaten at the last stop and, as Russell had suggested, tried a cheeseburger—very delicious. As were the french fries. But what had really bowled him over was the sweet drink called a Coca-cola. There were bubbles in it, and it was alive in his mouth! It went perfectly with the sandwich—very enjoyable. Russell had scolded him when he belched his delight loudly into the small café and instructed him to excuse himself. But he was beginning to really see why civilization was worth saving.

Now he was walking along the streets and enjoying the sights, sounds, and smells. Russell was again anticipating his questions and answering them. As Bill approached the destination building, only a few blocks from the train station, he saw that it was something called a Hotel.

"This is where you will be spending the night," Russell explained. "You will rent a room with a bed and a bathroom, much like what we had provided for you here."

Bill looked around and no one was nearby. "Okay, when will I complete the mission?" he asked.

"That will be tomorrow."

Bill stopped. "What? That soon?!"

"Yes, William. You're almost done."

Bill thought for a moment, then continued walking. "I don't even know what I'm supposed to do yet!"

"Yes, that is true. When you sleep tonight, I will give you much more of the background."

Bill put a hand to his head, which hurt quite a bit less now. "Oh, boy. Can't wait."

Russell said, "I'm sorry about that William. I have to be a little heavy-handed with you on this, there's no way around it. It's the same way I taught my engineers to build the MASS tanks and the Kronos. In fact, the whole city. Although with them I could dole out smaller increments. It's actually a very efficient way to communicate. Mankind will someday take it for granted...if all goes well tomorrow, that is. Which I'm sure it will."

Bill was still thinking this over when he reached the hotel entrance. Inside was a grand hall with a soft decorative floor. There were huge paintings on the walls, plush chairs, large indoor plants, and people were dressed very nicely. Under Russell's instruction, Bill approached the large desk with a well-groomed man standing behind it. He seemed to be concentrating completely on what he was writing in a large book. Bill cleared his throat quietly, and the man looked up at him. His face turned sour when he saw how Bill was dressed. Forcing himself to smile, he said, "May I help you...sir?"

Bill said, "I would like a room for the night please."

"I'm sorry, we're all booked up."

Bill seemed to be thinking solemnly, but was actually listening to Russell. He reached into his backpack and pulled out a large wad of money. Holding it up he said, "That's too bad. I guess I'll have to take my money somewhere else."

Then man's eyes widened and he looked around quickly. "Sir, please put that away. Give me a moment." He went into a room behind the desk, and Bill could hear him talking quietly to someone. Presently he returned. "Sir, I was incorrect earlier. We have a nice room for you on the eleventh floor."

"Thank you."

Bill settled up with the man behind the desk and was given a key. He walked to the elevators amidst some strange looks from people in the lobby. Pushing the button, he waited quietly until the doors opened. Once inside, he let out a sigh of relief at finally being alone again.

"Whew. I'm glad you're here to help me through this." He pushed the button marked "11."

"You're doing fine."

The elevator started moving, and Bill grabbed the rail.

"Not sure I'll ever get used to new stuff happening to me all the time." When the elevator stopped, the doors opened and he walked into the hallway and down to his room. He inserted the key into the lock and turned it. The door opened to a very large room with sizeable windows that looked out over the city. He stepped inside, looking around with his mouth agape. There was a huge bed with too many pillows, a similar soft decorative floor—carpet, Russell informed him—and more plush furniture to sit on. Some of the furnishings he didn't recognize. The bathroom was also huge, with a large tub and marble sinks. He put his things on the floor and walked around, taking it all in.

"Um…this is all for me?"

"Yes, William. I thought you should spend your last night of the mission in comfort."

"Well…maybe I could get used to *some* of the new stuff happening to me."

Chapter 60

"Star One to the unidentified MASS tank approaching from the southeast. Answer please." Ramey listened to the radio and grinned. He had made a stop near the river after driving through some particularly rough vegetation, trying to scratch up the hull as much as possible. At the river he had found some limestone rocks and had beaten on the outside of the tank, as well as made long white scratches in various directions—especially on the side with the door. Satisfied with his artwork, he continued on his way. Now the tank looked like it had seen some pretty rough action.

The manual had shown him just how far outside the city his tank could be detected, which he had determined to be the turn point. He wanted it to look like he was coming from the direction of the search and that they had somehow missed him. He was now moving at a considerably slower speed, trying to make the tank look crippled. On the view screen he saw the mound of the city approaching slowly.

"Star One to the unidentified MASS tank approaching from the southeast. Answer." Ramey continued to grin and drive. Then he heard, "This is Star One to all call. Cancel search operation and return to base. Repeat, cancel search and return to base. The bird is returning to the nest."

Ramey knew this was coming and also knew he had plenty of time. The other tanks wouldn't be here for almost an hour. The radio came to life again. "James are you able to communicate?" After a long pause, he flashed the tank's lights. "We have you on visual. When you get in, report directly to repair bays, unless you need immediate medical attention. If so, stop just inside and open her up."

Good. This was all he could hope for! They were going to open the doors and let him right in. From Ramey's previous visit to the city, he knew the repair bays were to the right about fifty yards inside the doors—perfect for what he had planned.

"Oh, I'll head for the repair bays all right, then I have a little surprise."

As he approached the bottom of the hill, the doors began to open. He drove somewhat erratically, as if he were having trouble controlling the vehicle. Once inside, he saw medical personnel standing by, but he turned toward the repair bays, and about halfway there slowed to a stop. He hit a few buttons on the engine controls, powering it up and down to add to the effect. He even opened the door a little way a couple of times, then closed it again and locked it. He could see on the monitors that mechanics were walking toward the tank. Finally he powered it down and sat there, waiting.

When the mechanics arrived, they knocked on the door. "You guys okay in there?" came muffled shouts.

Ramey did his best James impression, yelling, "Yeah, we're okay. A few bumps and bruises. Can you guys get us out?"

"Hang in there, we'll get you out in a jiffy."

"Not soon enough," Ramey said quietly.

He watched the mechanics send for tools and then examine the area around the door. He went to the battle position and powered it up. The ball on top of the tank was in perfect condition, and it began to rise. The mechanics were yelling and knocking on the door again. He targeted the doorway control area and fired. There was a man standing at the control panel and he fell into two pieces on the floor, his insides spilling out. There was a shower of sparks, and the only way in or out of the city was cut off.

He fired a few more shots in random directions and then shut the weapon off. He went to the door of the tank and knocked back.

Once again in his best James he yelled, "My God! Is everyone okay? Damn tank's got a mind of its own! We've pulled the plug on the weapon!"

Oh, this was just as fun as he had imagined!

Chapter 61

Bill was sitting in a pizza parlor, chewing on a slice of pepperoni pizza. He was at a corner table with no one nearby and was facing the wall. There was music playing over the speakers in the ceiling, and he was having an enjoyable time. He whispered to Russell, "I gotta tell you, if I save nothing else at all, this food will be worth all the trouble."

"Yes, William. Once again I am envious. That pizza you're eating is a great example of what a civilization can come up with if it works together. The meat comes from a ranch here in Texas, the cheese from Wisconsin, the tomatoes in the sauce from Louisiana, the spices from farms in the Midwest, and the wheat in the crust from Kansas. All these ingredients come together through a system of agreements to deliver them here or other restaurants. In exchange, the farmers and ranchers get money. Without this system...without society...you get what you just came from. Imagine trying to put a pizza together here. Our chefs have tried, but it was severely lacking."

Bill listened to all this as he finished his last slice. He paid the man at the register, including what he had now learned was a generous "tip," and walked out. He was carrying his backpack only, having left the case in the room. It was dusk when he had entered the restaurant, but as he walked outside there was no light left except for that emitted by an occasional street lamp or neon sign.

"Now William, I need you to do something. Let's take a little walk."

Under Russell's instruction, Bill walked a few blocks among the buildings. Finally Russell said, "Now walk across this parking lot and toward that street." He did so, seeing the street was a downhill slope between two embankments. There were almost no cars out, and he felt he was alone. "Walk a little way along the street toward that underpass." He did so, though there was no sidewalk near the road. "Now stop. Next to the curb I need you to dig a hole. There's a gardening trowel in your backpack. Make sure you cut the sod and pick it up in one piece." Russell sent a little mental image of what Bill was supposed to do. Bill complied. "Good. Now drop one of the three stones in and replace the sod. You'll need to repeat this for the other two as well. I'll show you where."

When Bill had finished, he noted that with two stones on one side of the street and one on the other, they created a triangular shape. "Is this where—"

"Yes, William. You are to return here tomorrow and complete the mission."

"Which you will show me more about tonight?"

"Exactly."

Bill looked around, memorizing the area. It was only a short walk from the hotel. "Guess I should head back now."

"Yes, you will need to go to sleep. I will...just a moment...I need to leave you for now William. Apparently there's some trouble here I need to attend to. I will return after you ready yourself for sleep. Try to relax in the meantime. You'll need your rest."

"Is everything okay?"

There was no answer. Bill waited for a few more seconds, then turned toward the hotel and began to walk.

Chapter 62

When Russell settled into his body, Ellen was there waiting for him. "Russell you must come quickly, there's been an accident." He followed her out of his room and toward the entrance of the city.

"Was anyone hurt?"

"Yes, one of the workers was killed. It was Edward Templeton."

"Oh my. You were right to call me back."

"It was a malfunctioning tank. It had been through some kind of rough activity and was brought in for repairs. The weapon deployed without warning and fired."

"That doesn't seem very likely," Russell said, quickening his pace. "I'll have to investigate more closely."

When they arrived at the open area near the entrance, Russell looked at the tank. He quickly sat down and "moved" into the tank.

Immediately, Ramey could sense his brother's presence and turned toward him with a smile.

"Hello, brother. About time you got here." His voice was filled with venom.

Russell sped back to his body and raised his hand toward the tank. It started to levitate off the floor and then slammed back down.

"It's my brother!" he said to Ellen. He sent a telepathic message to the safety crew to man the internal weapons. "Cover that tank, but do not fire!" He also sent a message to the mechanics around the tank to run and take cover, as he and Ellen were also doing behind some barriers.

After a few seconds, three lasers were pointed at the tank, ready to fire. They were aimed to avoid the nuclear reactor but would disable the drive and the weapon. Russell sensed his brother had left his body and the tank. He tried to levitate the tank again, but his brother was holding it down.

"Well Ramey, it looks like we're at a bit of a standoff."

Ramey's reply was not as pleasant. "You're defense system is full of holes. I'm here now, and it's time for you to surrender. Just hand over the city and no one has to be hurt."

"Come, come, now. Is that any way to talk to your only brother? Besides, if I get hurt you will too." He sent a message to one of the gunners, and a laser fired at the tank. It pierced the hull and cut through one of the axles, missing his brother's body. The tank shuddered and dropped slightly on one end.

"Okay, stop that! I'm coming out." Russell could sense him going back into the tank. Shortly the door opened and Ramey emerged with his hands over his head. He did not have a look of defeat on his face, instead it was mostly neutral with a touch of cunning.

"Keep those weapons trained on him. If I give the command, kill him." This message was sent to the weapons controllers and to Ramey. He beckoned more guards and sent Ellen back to her office.

Ramey bellowed, "Okay, you got me brother!"

When the guards arrived and their rifles were on the brute, Russell walked with them to take his brother to a holding room. His senses were attuned to anything Ramey might do, but he seemed compliant for now.

"Don't worry brother, I won't try anything. I just want to talk." Russell didn't reply.

"I respect the beating I took on the battlefield, and I just want to come to an understanding." There was still no reply. After a bit he continued.

"Nice place you got here. All the creature comforts from before the war. I bet you have a lot of good-looking women, too! That one you had standing next to you back there wasn't too bad. What *is* too bad is that you don't have any tools on that little body to work her over with!" Russell ignored his brother's taunts.

They had arrived at the holding room. Inside was a table with two chairs across from each other. There was also a simple bed and a toilet, but that was all. Everything was white, and the soft light once again seemed to come from nowhere and everywhere. Ramey stopped at the door, looked around the room, and whistled.

"Just for me?" His amazement was obviously exaggerated. He stood there with his hairy eyebrows raised, as if waiting for an invitation.

189

"After you, dear brother," Russell finally spoke telepathically so that everyone there could hear.

"Why thank you!" Ramey said aloud and bowed, before entering the room. He pulled out a chair and sat heavily down with a pleased look on his face. Russell moved his own chair out with a wave of his hand and sat opposite his hulk of a brother. The guards had entered the room as well, with their weapons still on Ramey.

"Are they necessary?"

Russell sat down and looked at his brother steadily. "Yes, quite."

For the first time since he emerged from the tank, Ramey looked displeased.

"I kind of hoped we could have a private conversation."

"I can speak so that no one but you hears," he said to Ramey only.

"Yeah, I never quite got the hang of talking to these idiots, you know?" Ramey said out loud. "At least not without destroying whoever I was talking to." He smiled at the guards.

"That's too bad, but you don't have to worry. You're not quite strong enough to hurt me."

"Okay, bro. Just you and me," Ramey said telepathically.

"You may not be able to overpower me, but you did catch me by surprise and destroy part of my mind. That was a mistake on my part that I'm not willing to make again. The guards and their weapons stay."

There was a knock at the door. A man was standing there holding a strange-looking helmet.

"Sir, you requested this?"

"Yes," said Russell, "please bring it in." The man did. "Place it on my brother's head." The man started to but Ramey protested.

"Wait, what the hell is this?" he asked out loud, ducking his head and putting up his arms.

Russell looked at him steadily with his large eyes. He spoke slowly but loudly into his brother's mind. "If you want to live, you will put on the helmet." The guards took a step closer and acted as if they would shoot him right then and there.

Ramey looked at the guards and then back at his brother. Slowly he put his hands down, and a smile spread across his face. When he spoke it was telepathically.

"Brother, you have impressed me again."

Chapter 63

Bill sat in his hotel room watching TV. It had taken him a while to figure out how it worked, but he finally got it going—even figured out how to work the volume. He had no idea there were two other channels to choose from.

"Hello, William."

Bill had been absorbed in watching the local news, and Russell's voice startled him. "Whoa! There you are."

"Yes. I thought I'd give you some time to relax and recover. There's been some trouble at home."

"Everything okay?"

"Just my brother, making himself a nuisance again. Nothing I couldn't handle. I had my engineers build a little device that keeps his abilities in check. He's quite harmless now and locked away."

"Well, that's good...I guess. If you had him that close, why didn't you just kill him and be done with it?"

"I have my reasons. There is a chance you will fail this mission, I'm afraid, albeit a small one. If so, we're stuck with the world the way it is now. He is my brother, and I'm hoping he can be...adjusted let's call it. If so, he could be a powerful assistant. We would still try to save the human race as it is now, but the endeavor would be doubtful at best."

Bill thought about this. He also thought about what had happened to his family. "Well, I can't help but hope you end up killing him—and not in a pleasant way."

"I understand your feelings. Now, to the task at hand. I need you to lie down on the bed."

Bill got up and turned off the TV. "Wait...I was watching the news and they said something about an important man visiting..."

"Yes, William, I know what you're going to ask. Your mission has everything to do with that visit. Now lie down, and I'll show you more of what you need to know."

Bill lay on the bed and made himself comfortable. He was about to ask another question, but instead went unconscious.

* * *

He was instantly floating through blurry images again and felt himself moving toward the one clear one and then dropping in.

He was back in the Soviet Union but knew that years had passed since his last experience. He was in a schoolyard, and there was Andrei, much older now. He was being picked on by some bigger boys who were taunting him—something about being too smart for his own good. Bill "knew" he had been doing very well in school. This had caused extra homework to be assigned by his teacher, and the boys were turning their anger on him. They had him surrounded. Some of them were carrying sticks, and others were picking up rocks.

Once again, Vasily came to his rescue. He was quite a bit bigger now and had put on some muscle. Charging in, he began taking on the crowd of boys. They tried to fight him, but were no match. He punched a couple, and they fell, then the others took off running. When they were all gone, he put his arm around his younger brother and asked in that strange language, "You okay?"

Andrei answered, "No. If you hadn't come along they might have killed me. This has been building for a while. I don't mean to make them so angry, I just do my best at school and look what it gets me. Maybe I should just be dumb like them."

Vasily turned to face him. "Now you listen to me. You're smart—very smart. That's a gift, and you're not going to piss it away because of those idiots. You're going to be somebody big in the party some day and all these ants will be groveling at your feet. Including me." Andrei looked up at his brother and smiled. His brother returned his smile. "Now come, let's see what Ma has cooked us for dinner."

Bill popped out of this scene and floated to another.

* * *

Several years had passed again, and he was at a military ceremony. Vasily was a grown young man now and was graduating from military training. He was joining the infantry in the Soviet Army. His mother and younger brother were in the audience with smiles on their faces. He also knew Yuri had died of a liver disorder some years before.

* * *

Now he was at another ceremony several years later. This time Andrei was graduating from an Eastern European university. Bill once again "knew" that he was graduating with an honors degree in nuclear physics. His mother was in the audience alone while his brother was away serving in the Army.

* * *

Bill was getting a bit dizzy, moving through space and time without warning. Now he was in the Oval Office of the White House. The president, Kennedy was his name, was signing a paper in front of other men in suits. It was for something very important by the look of things. Again he instantly knew that it was the order for a military invasion into a country called Cuba.

* * *

Bill finally woke up in his room. He hadn't moved since lying down, but there was something warm and sticky on the right side of his face. He put his hand there and winced.

"William, are you all right?"

Bill took stock of himself. "Well, I have one hell of a headache—and a nosebleed to boot. Not to mention my shoulder and back are killing me. But other than that, I'm fine."

"I'm sorry, William, but this is all necessary."

Bill slowly got up and went to the bathroom, grabbing a towel to put to his nose. He looked at himself in the mirror and saw that he looked even worse than he felt. There were heavy, dark bags under his eyes, and his skin looked pale. Finally he walked back to the bed and sat down. "I remember everything you were showing me, but I still don't know what I'm supposed to do."

"There is more to show you, but I'll have to do it slowly. Lie back down and I'll let you sleep for now. I'll show you the rest before your task tomorrow. You have a big day coming up and you'll need your strength. I'm afraid saving the world is very hard work."

Chapter 64

Ramey was furious. How could he have let this happen? He sat on the small bed in his holding cell with armed guards outside his door. The stupid helmet his brother had put on him was worse than a prison. Every time he tried to go outside of his body, he felt searing, intense pain in his head—same for trying to move objects. Normally he figured he could take any pain his brother could dish out, but this was blinding. He had tried taking it off, but it was locked on with a chinstrap, and any pressure on it also caused agony. If he sat quietly and didn't try anything, at least the pain would subside considerably, only leaving a dull ache behind.

Russell appeared in the doorway, standing and observing his brother silently.

Ramey turned his hateful gaze toward his brother. "You son of a bitch. Take this thing off me!"

"I'm afraid that wouldn't be wise." Russell spoke to him telepathically, and it didn't cause any discomfort. "I constructed this helmet with you in mind brother, for just such an occasion as this. As long as you remain docile, there will be no pain."

Ramey regarded Russell for a while and then smiled. "I got to hand it to you. I never figured you for something like this. You were always the peaceful one. But I see your tanks in action killing my men, and your guards clearly wouldn't hesitate to kill me. Now this pain machine you made for me. You're just full of surprises, aren't you."

"As are you. You actually had me fooled into thinking you were dead for a while. I thought maybe you had something to do with that dog seeing a bear, but I still couldn't find you. I thought for a while that I must have been mistaken. You hide yourself well."

"It wasn't easy." Ramey looked around the room. "Well, what now brother?"

"Now we see about your rehabilitation. If you're going to live here peacefully, we have to see about changing your mind about some things."

"Peacefully? Peacefully. My dear Russell, do you know me at all?"

"I know what you're capable of, yes. I've been in your mind, as uncomfortable as that was. You're convinced that taking from others is the only way to survive. But I also know you have potential. The hard part will be bringing that out in you. Right now all you understand is pain."

Ramey sat there with his mouth agape, staring at Russell. Finally he started laughing—boisterously. Russell waited patiently.

When his mirth subsided, he found his voice again. "You...you think you can change me? Boy, you are crazy."

"Perhaps. But the alternative to change is, of course...death."

That took the smile off Ramey's face. He got up and started toward Russell, and instantly the pain was back. He put his hands to the helmet and stumbled back to his bed, sitting down hard. The pain stopped, and once again he glared at his brother.

"You see, the helmet is attuned to my mind as well. I can cause you agony with a single thought."

Ramey's voice cracked as he spoke, "How...how did you build this thing. I mean how did you know...how?"

"With the help of some friends from across the galaxy. You see Ramey, while you were concentrating on your own pleasures and causing pain in others, I was working on traveling and exploring. I discovered my friends, or rather they discovered me, while I was in another part of the galaxy observing a celestial event. It was a supernova. They were there to watch too, and we struck up a conversation. I told them about how we had destroyed ourselves and how we were doomed as a species. They are much more advanced than we are, and they decided to help me. With the technology they gave me, primitive by their standards, we can fix this. We can make the world better and save mankind from extinction."

Ramey sat there and took all this in. "There's the Russell I know. Always trying to fix things and make it better for others. You must be miserable."

"On the contrary. I am very much at peace with my followers here and the universe as a whole. It is an immense pleasure you have never even come close

197

to knowing."

"Sounds like a lot of bullshit to me. Give me a good woman to play with, and I'll show you what pleasure is."

Russell regarded him solemnly. "I can see we have a long way to go. Rest here, and I'll be back to help you as much as I can." He turned and left his brother in his cell.

Ramey yelled after him, "Yeah, you can have fun tryin'!" He lay back on his bed and tried to get comfortable with the bulky helmet on. His brother had surprised him again and again, and his plans had gone to hell. Now he would just have to come up with a new one. And he knew he would.

Chapter 65

"One down, two left," Russell said. Bill complied by turning the scope site adjustments.

Bill had awakened in the dark hours of the morning from a restless sleep, feeling little better than when Russell had left him. He took a shower and ordered room service by following the instructions on a card by the phone. The pancakes made him feel a little better, but they weren't as good as the ones from the diner. The pain in his head made everything he did more difficult.

Soon after eating, Russell had rejoined him and told him to open the case he had been carrying since he left the Kronos. It had a combination lock on it, to which Russell had supplied the code. When he opened it, Bill's breath caught in his throat. Inside was a rifle, broken down into a barrel with a mounted scope and a stock. It was a caliber he wasn't familiar with, a 6.5mm Mannlicher Carcano, according to Russell. The rifle was custom made with camouflage paint covering it and was equipped with a single clip containing three shells. The rifle parts were set into foam rubber padding with customized indentations. Bill had assembled the rifle easily with a single locked in hand screw, and now he was sighting it in with Russell's help.

Normally he would have gone to a secluded place and fired, but time wouldn't allow for that. He was only a few hours away from go time. Plus, they had only given him three shells. So Russell instructed him to aim the scope out the window to a point across the street from the hotel, and then he would move inside the barrel and look out. That way he was able to see where the rifle was actually pointed, instead of where Bill was looking, and tell Bill what adjustments to make. Then they would repeat the process. It was raining lightly, but the window was dry.

"One more down and that should do it," Russell told him. Bill made the adjustment and targeted the point, which was a red dot on an Indian woman's head. Her portrait was part of a rooftop billboard advertising travel to foreign lands. "See the world," it said, "let us show you how!"

"Yes, that is spot on," Russell told him. "Now I need you to lie down, and I'll give you more of the mission background."

Bill put the rifle down across the open case and asked, "Really? I have to go through more of that? Can't you just tell me who I have to kill? I assume that's why I'm here…to kill someone."

"It's not that easy, William. If you don't have the entire background; you may hesitate. Then all would be lost."

"I'll do whatever you ask. I know what's at stake now. I don't want to do that background thing anymore."

"You see, you're already disagreeing with me. There can be no doubt when it comes to mission completion, and we can't take any chances."

Bill thought this over. "I guess you know better than me." He stood and stretched, wincing again at the pain in his shoulder and arm. After walking to his bed and standing there looking down at it for a moment, a heavy sigh shuddered from him. He lay down and was immediately unconscious.

* * *

Bill was on a tropical island he knew to be called Cuba. He was watching a firefight between the American and Cuban soldiers. Alongside the Cubans was a foreign soldier he now knew was brought in to instruct the natives on the Soviet way of fighting. He recognized this man as Vasily. He watched as the Russian yelled instructions at the Cuban soldiers in Spanish. They were doing what he said and seemed to be winning the firefight. A small number of them charged forward in the jungle and engaged the Americans from a closer position. This did not please Vasily, and he stood to shout at them.

Bill's attention was then focused on an American soldier who aimed at the Russian and fired. The bullet caught Vasily in the chest and pierced his heart. The Russian fell to the ground and in a matter of seconds was dead.

* * *

Now Bill was in a lab in the Soviet Union. Several men in white lab coats were working on weapons. He knew these were nuclear warheads and they were being prepared to receive their deadly fuel cores. An announcement came over a speaker system asking one of them to report to an administrative office. The message was for the scientist named Andrei. He walked out of the lab and to the office, quite obviously not knowing what to expect. When he arrived, he was asked to sit down. The news was grave. His brother had been killed in Cuba by an invading American force. The details were in a letter that was handed to him. Thanks in no small part to his brother's heroic efforts, the capitalists had been defeated.

He was sent home for the day, but Bill knew he would read that letter over and over, until it became frayed. And each time Andrei read it, he would become more certain that this could not be ignored. His brother had stood up for him so many times, just to be cut down in his prime by those smug Americans. He must do something.

* * *

Bill was now in an office a few weeks later, and Andrei was requesting that he be allowed to accompany the warheads to their forward destination—closer to the United States than any other missiles had ever been placed. His carefully planned speech convinced the government superiors and they approved the order. Andrei was going to Cuba.

Chapter 66

Ramey was eating a meal of chicken and vegetables—very tasty. *This,* he thought to himself, *is what it should be like always.* And the cup of water he was given was so clean. And very sweet. His brother sure had it good here.

He had come up with another plan and was going to execute it as soon as he finished his last bite. Knowing for sure now that he could hide from his brother was very important to his new plan, and soon enough he would be free to disappear into the darkest places of this city.

After he finished eating, he yelled, "Done!" and lay back on his bed.

Shortly one of the staff, a female he was pleased to see, appeared in the doorway and walked toward the tray. Immediately he jumped up and grabbed her, knocking the tray and its contents to the floor. There was no pain in his head, indicating his brother was unaware of his actions, at least for the moment. The two armed guards rushed into the room, and he placed the young woman in front of him as a shield. Moving around the room with her, he soon had a blank wall to his back.

He looked at the guards and said, "One step closer and I snap her neck!" They stopped, about eight feet away. "Good, now stay right there." Another part of his plan was dependent on the helmet's complexity and therefore its fragility. He bent forward with the girl in front of him and reared his head into the wall as hard as he could. In addition to seeing stars from the impact, he heard buzzing and snapping from inside the helmet.

There was a bright flash of pain and then nothing. He had done it! Concentrating on the rifles pointed at him, he used his abilities to first pinch the barrels shut, then fold them back. Still there was no pain. The guards looked at their rifles with astonishment.

Ramey threw the girl to the side, and the guard's bodies shot up to the ceiling, smashing into it, and then fell unconscious to the floor. The girl was also out on the floor, probably from her impact with the wall. Ramey broke the strap on his helmet and then took it off and threw it on the bed, crushing it with his mind. He peeked out the door and looked around. "Too easy," he said quietly and ran. His brother must have been occupied somewhere else. *Probably traipsing around the galaxy or something.*

After a bit he found a blind alleyway with trashcans in it and sat on the ground behind them. No one had seen him enter the alley, and it was nice and dark in here. He just needed a few minutes undisturbed. He crossed his legs and left his body.

Traveling up near the top of the underside of the hill, he surveyed the city below. He saw that they had opened the main doorway and some tanks were coming in. His destroyed tank had been moved to the side, over near the wall. He also saw a work area in the center of the city with a pad of some kind and moved in closer. There were control panels with cables running to the pad, but whatever they had been working on was gone. *Interesting.*

He moved back up and continued searching. Finding more cables and conduit, he followed them. They all seemed to be coming from one dome-shaped building not far from the pad. *Ah*, he thought, *that's got to be it.*

Moving down inside the domed structure, he observed several workers sitting at complicated control panels, watching dials and gauges. It was kind of noisy in here with a steady hum. This had to be the source of their power. He looked around for the center from which the noise was emanating and saw another smaller dome. Wanting to learn as much as he could, he tried to move inside it. Pain! Quickly he moved out and stopped. How could this be? He had never felt pain while outside his body! It must be some kind of energy that could hurt his very being! Damn those friends of his brother's. No matter. He looked over the controls and was satisfied he could shut it all down from out here when the time came.

Quickly he moved back to his body and opened his eyes. Why hadn't his brother detected him yet? *Must be busy doing something. Something stupid, no doubt.* Oh well, he needed to go to a more comfortable place to hide and thought he knew just the spot.

Chapter 67

Bill tried to open his eyes but found that they were stuck shut. He brought his fingers to them and felt a crusted layer that he was able to wipe carefully away, and only then could he force his lids open. The sides of his face were wet as well—more blood.

He felt horrible. He could only guess how he must look.

"I'm sorry William. I'm feeding this information to you as gently as I can, but apparently it's a bit much for you."

Bill found his voice, but it sounded like it came from a dried up toad. "It's not so bad," he croaked. Taking it very slowly, he managed to sit up. He glanced at his blood-stained pillow, then tried to stand. He fell back on the bed after the first try, immensely dizzy. After a bit, his head cleared and he tried again. "Okay, a little bad," he said as he stood.

"There's only a little more, but I'll wait for you to recover some. Go ahead and clean up, then I need for you to take your belongings here." He pushed an image of exactly where Bill was supposed to go, close to where he had buried the stones.

Bill winced at the additional data, then said, "Got it."

He walked over to the bathroom and turned on the water before looking up into the mirror. When he did, he gasped. Before him stood a reflection of a man who had been beaten badly. There were dark circles around his eyes, blood all over his face, and he was uncharacteristically slouched. But the eyes themselves were the worst. They were very clear, as if they didn't belong in the mess surrounding them. At least his nose had stopped bleeding—for now. He tried to stand up straight and winced at the sharp pain in his shoulder that radiated down his back and to his butt. Nope, that didn't feel right at all.

"It's the cancer," Russell said. "Spreading rapidly now."

"Oh, well. At least I got that going for me." Bill's sarcasm was a good sign, and he surprised even himself.

"Glad to see you have some life in you. Now, I have to leave you for a while. It would appear my brother's been up to no good back home while I've been busy with you here."

"I thought you could jump around anywhere in time. Can't you just go to before he did something?"

"Doesn't quite work that way. I can visit you at any point in this time, but while I'm here with you my timeline is continuing back home as always. Anyway, do you think you can make it to where I showed you on your own?"

Bill sighed shakily and said, "Yeah, pretty sure I can. Just hope I don't have to run there."

"No, we still have time. But don't delay too long. You're almost done William, just a few more tasks. I'll meet you when you get there."

"Okay, hurry back."

There was no reply, and he knew Russell had left him.

* * *

Bill had cleaned up his face and changed into his one remaining set of clothes from the backpack. After disassembling the rifle, he packed up his meager belongings and opened the door to the room. He stood there for a moment, taking a lingering look back. How easy would it be to just forget this so-called mission and live out the rest of his short life here in this luxurious room? To just drop his things and go lie down again, close his eyes, lay his weary head on one of the still-clean pillows, and just sleep until blessed death finally came for him? *Too damn easy, that's how.*

With another shaky sigh he turned and closed the door behind him as he headed unsteadily toward the elevator.

Chapter 68

Ramey had found this spot when he had been hovering above the city before. It was well-hidden, warm, and very comfortable. Apparently when the laundry became torn or too worn to use, it was dumped behind the building where they washed their clothes. There was a mound of it higher than his head leaned up against the wall, and it was in another blind alley. Smelled a little, but he'd been in much worse conditions. No way they would find his body here while he looked around some more.

He buried himself in the linens with only part of his face exposed and left his body. Hovering above the city again, he noticed this time he wasn't alone. *Damn.*

"Hello, Ramey. I see you've been busy."

Ramey rushed at him, not sure what he could do in this form. As it turned out, not much at all.

"Where's your body, brother?" Russell asked. After a moment he said, "And what exactly are you up to now?"

Ramey was eager to reply, "Oh, stick around and you'll see! You're gonna die today!"

"Oh, I'm sure I will soon enough. But of course, so will you by the look of that tumor in your lung. Yes, I noticed when we had our little talk before. I guess we're both mortal after all."

Ramey, furious now, "Tell me brother, where's *your* body?!"

"Oh, well protected I assure you. I'm afraid you won't be able to harm me as easily as you thought."

"We'll see about that!" and Ramey moved away quickly, searching frantically for his brother's body. Shifting rapidly through the buildings with no luck, he was starting to wonder if Russell's body was even here. Then he spotted the young woman who had been with Russell before. She was walking with a little girl toward the opening of the hill. He rushed into her head and looked around.

He learned that her name was Ellen and her daughter's name was Sarah. She was six. Then he also saw where her boss, Russell, usually went to leave his body. He left her head and she dropped to the ground, unconscious and convulsing. He barely noticed Sarah's screams as he went to where Russell's body was. Sure enough, there it was in a room, cross-legged and floating above the floor. He also noticed his brother was in the room with him.

"That wasn't a very nice thing you did to Ellen. I'm afraid we can't keep you here anymore. You're much too dangerous. I've already dispatched troops to search for your body, and they have orders to kill it when it's found. This room is heavily guarded, and you'll never get in here to kill mine. I'm afraid you've brought this all on yourself, brother."

Ramey left the room and was instantly back to his body so his brother couldn't follow, and he re-entered it. He stood quickly and thought for a moment, tracing out a map in his memory. *Damn!* He was still too far from where he needed to be.

He crept to the edge of the alleyway and peered around the corner. He could see groups of armed men searching every square inch of the place. It was only a matter of time before they found him anyway. He had to get out of here before his brother found him. He could feel him searching as well, high above the city.

A MASS tank was coming slowly down one of the roadways that passed the alley. *Perfect.* He crouched down and waited, still hidden. When it finally got even with the alley, he kept low and ran to get under one side of it. It was moving slowly enough he could keep up with little effort, and it was going in the direction he wanted to go.

Soon he was next to the building he had targeted earlier. He was somewhat exposed here, but he ran next to the building and stopped, once more closing his eyes. It was the domed building near the center of the city, and he pictured the control panels inside. He used his abilities to crush them one by one.

Inside the building, sparks spouted from the boxes as they collapsed. To the workers it looked like an invisible hand was crushing them, and they began running out the doors and away from the building.

Russell had spotted Ramey and directed the soldiers toward his location, but they were still some distance away.

A computerized voice sounded loud enough for the whole city to hear.

"Warning. Nuclear containment controls offline, core meltdown probable. Evacuate the city immediately."

"Oh, Ramey. What have you done?" Russell asked inside his head.

"Just shutting off your power." The lights began to flicker and a high-pitched hum started to come from the building.

"I'm afraid you've done much more than that. If you wanted to destroy this city, then your mission is accomplished."

"*No!* I want this city for myself! You've got it good here, and I wanted to live what little life I have left in comfort."

"I would have allowed that if you had just cooperated."

People were rushing toward the hill opening, and the lights continued to flicker. The hum was getting louder, and some pieces of the underside of the hill were falling all around Ramey as he watched the results of shutting down the power. This wasn't what he wanted. "Why is this place falling—"

The computer voice interrupted him. "Warning. Core meltdown imminent. Evacuate the city immediately."

"What does that mean? Why is everybody running out?"

"You've destroyed the only way to control the power source to this city. I'm afraid the hill is too large for me to hold up, and I can't shield you and these people from falling debris. That power source was holding up the hill above the city. And thanks to you, now it's failing."

"Well shit! You should've—"

At that moment, a large chunk of dirt and rock fell on Ramey, knocking him to the ground. Dazed, he looked up to see daylight peeking through several patches of the hill's underside, with more coming through steadily.

"I'm going to leave you now, brother. You're going to die here today, and at your own hand. But I suppose it's of some consolation to you that you've killed most of us too. Including me." And then Russell was silent.

"Wait! Don't just leave me here!" Larger chunks were falling now and hitting people as they ran toward the opening.

Ramey tried to get up and made it as far as a low crouch, but another piece hit his back and knocked him flat on his stomach. He rolled over and was about to try again when he looked up. The rock was about three feet across, shaped like a potato, and falling straight toward him. He tried to stop it with his mind but only managed to slow it slightly, and it fell across his hips and thighs, crushing them without bouncing. He screamed in agony. After a moment, he managed to lift the rock away with telekinesis, and strangely enough there was no pain this time—probably because his back was broken too. He was bleeding very badly from one thigh.

So this was how it was going to end for him.

He tried to stop the hill from collapsing on him any further but only managed to create a dome around himself, deflecting the debris. Soon it piled up over his mini-dome shield, and he was in darkness. His life was slipping away in a pulsing stream from a crushed leg. All his work and the good things he had done, undone by his stupid brother. He could feel unconsciousness sweeping over him now and knew there wasn't anything else he could do. In one final effort, he tried to push the rubble away, but it was too heavy. He blacked out and his dome collapsed.

Chapter 69

When Bill arrived at the spot Russell had pointed him to, he was exhausted.

It had stopped raining, and he had taken several rest stops on the way—even going into a store to buy a candy bar. This act had been inspired by a young boy emerging from the store with one in hand, seeming to enjoy it immensely. While Bill was paying for the candy, the clerk had been staring at him. He knew he looked bad, but hoped the man wouldn't call the authorities. Bill thought about one of the movies he had seen and improvised.

"Car accident."

It had worked and he left the store. He stopped at a bench and tore open the wrapper. He had taken one bite, but it was overpoweringly sweet. He threw the remainder into a nearby garbage can and resumed walking, but the aftertaste was very good and he regretted discarding it. Too tired to go back and retrieve it, let alone buy another one, he continued on his way.

Now he was in the spot Russell had shown him, which was a cozy place between a picket fence and a large bush at the edge of the parking lot near the street, and he sat down. He was so relieved he didn't have to walk anymore.

"Hello William. I see you made it here okay."

"Yeah, easy as you please."

"Good. I have some bad news to tell you before we start. I'm afraid my brother has destroyed the city. He killed most of the people there. A few lucky ones did get out. You were right, I should have killed him when I had the chance."

"Oh, no. I'm so sorry...wait...are you okay?"

"I'm afraid he killed my body as well. But at least he is now dead with the rest of us."

"Wait. I don't understand. How can you be here now?"

"I only needed that body to manipulate my environment. I can no longer do that. I can, however, stay here with you long enough to complete my part of the mission. But just that long, and we must hurry. My body was also anchoring me to this general vicinity of the universe. Without it, it takes a great deal of effort to stay around."

Bill thought for a moment. He had a million questions but knew they must wait. He hid his belongings within the bush next to him and lay down in the grass and closed his eyes. To anyone passing who happened to see him, which wasn't likely, he would look like a sleeping vagrant.

"Okay, I'm ready."

"Good. These last bits are of utmost importance. So we begin."

* * *

Bill saw that he was here in the same place but a little later in the day. He looked but didn't see himself behind the fence. There were many people lining the street just up by the buildings. They were more scattered closer to his spot and across the street in a park, but they were all looking in the same direction—up the street away from him, or where he would be. Then he saw what they were looking at. A group of cars and what he now knew to be motorcycles were approaching at a relatively slow speed. The lead car seemed to be the focus of everyone's attention, and there were several people in it. A man in the back was waving to the people and sitting next to a woman. He was smiling. It was the same man he had seen signing the document giving the go-ahead to invade Cuba—the one the news had said was visiting the city today: Kennedy.

As his car approached a corner where it was about to turn, Bill heard a shot from the building. He saw a man sitting in one of the upper windows aiming a rifle. People looked around but must have not realized what had made that loud boom.

The car turned the corner and started down the street toward his spot. Kennedy was still waving. Then there was another loud boom. Kennedy grabbed his throat, and the man in the front seat had obviously been hit as well. The car continued toward the underpass and sped up.

* * *

Now Bill was in a hospital waiting room with a lot of people. Everyone was talking at the same time. A few were trying to comfort the woman from the car, who was crying. Some doors opened, and a small group of doctors and nurses walked in. Everyone got louder, and lights were flashing as reporters took pictures. The group approached where the woman was sitting, and one of the men wearing a suit and standing next to the woman yelled, *"Quiet!"* in a commanding voice. The crowd quickly quieted down.

Then one of the men from the group of doctors sat beside where the woman was sitting and said to her, "Mrs. Kennedy, the president lost some blood, but the bullet missed his spine and carotid artery. He'll have to go through some painful therapy for several months, but he should make a full recovery."

A heavy sigh emitted from the crowd, and then they began cheering.

* * *

Bill was now in Cuba at a military briefing. It was in Spanish but being translated into Russian as well to accommodate the audience members. They were talking about the Kennedy assassination attempt. Andrei sat in the back. He was brooding.

* * *

Now it was a few months later and he was in a plane over the Atlantic ocean at night, flying along the East Coast of the United States. It was on the approved route between Cuba and the Soviet Union.

Andrei was there too. He was escorting some nuclear warheads that Bill knew the Americans had ordered removed from Cuba. Most of them had been taken by ship over a year earlier, but the Americans didn't know about these. They were kept back just in case their adversaries pulled something again, and Andrei was their caretaker. These were the last two.

Andrei was showing no emotion as he looked down at the other three passengers. They were dead on the floor of the aircraft with their throats slit.

Andrei cleaned his knife on the last one's clothes and walked toward the pilot's cabin.

This was a type of Soviet cargo plane that Andrei had flown in many times before. He had often requested to sit in the cockpit when the plane took off and landed and had asked many questions about flying it. That had given him enough knowledge to get this job done.

He opened the door and was greeted by the navigator, whose eyes widened when he saw the blood on Andrei's lab coat. Andrei stabbed him in the neck. Then he stepped forward and stabbed the pilot in the same spot in his neck. The co-pilot was wearing a sidearm but was too slow, and Andrei killed him as well. He was now alone on the plane. The aircraft began to gently dive, but Andrei quickly removed the pilot and took the controls. He stabilized it and put it on autopilot.

He got up and turned to the navigation charts, checking his position—almost time. He walked back to where the warheads were stored and hooked up some wiring to a panel on the side of the one closest to the front. He had been clandestinely prepping the device for detonation prior to killing the three other passengers.

He connected a spool of wire to the panel and unrolled it to reach the cockpit. Once there, he carefully and slowly connected another device to the wire. It was a small box with batteries and a red button, which he set aside. He put on some headphones and tuned the radio.

With a heavy Russian accent, he said in English, "Mayday, Mayday. This is Soviet transport seven-five-seven-two-one reporting engine trouble. Request landing at nearest airport." He waited a bit and then repeated the message. After the third time he got a reply.

"Soviet transport seven-five-seven-two-one, this is Andrews Air Force Base control tower. Turn to course two-eight-seven and approach. Escort fighters have been scrambled. Follow their lead and do not deviate. Do you understand?"

"Understood, Andrews." He repeated the instructions and told them he would comply.

When the fighters arrived, they positioned themselves on either side of the transport. Andrei had already stopped one of the four prop engines to add to the effect. It seemed to be working. They were taking him directly toward Washington, D.C.

He approached per their instructions, but when it came time to land, he came in too high. He was instructed to come around and try again. Just as he had planned. He accelerated and made a left turn, gaining a little altitude. But instead of continuing around, he headed for the lights of the capitol city. The fighters, who had broken off to allow him to land, regrouped and began pursuit. The radio crackled. "Soviet transport! Return to runway approach! Resistance will result in use of deadly force!"

He replied, "I am having trouble with rudder, do not shoot at us!" He only needed a few more seconds.

"Soviet transport, you must turn around or you will be fired upon!"

"Please do not. We are trying to turn her!"

It was almost time. He could see the well-lit monuments beginning to pass below him, and his target was just ahead. He picked up the box with the red button.

He could hear a noise from behind the aircraft and then saw the tracer fire pass him on his right side.

They were warning him.

He smiled.

His plane was over the Whitehouse now.

He whispered, "For Vasily," and pressed the button.

* * *

The president and his wife were asleep in their bedroom. His bedside phone rang and he sat up, knowing only a national crisis would cause that phone to ring.

He heard planes flying outside, rather low.

He heard machinegun fire.

Then his world turned white.

* * *

214

"William, wake up. It's almost time."

Bill tried to open his eyes, but once again they were stuck shut. He felt even worse than before. Trying to raise his hands to remove the gunk, he had to let them drop to his side again. With tremendous effort, he managed to get his fingers to his eyes and finally got them open. Warm wetness was on his face again. He felt like he had been trampled by a herd of horses.

He tried to speak and managed, "Uhhhgn."

"William, I'm so sorry. All this was necessary. You now know what you must do and why you've been brought here to this place and moment in time. I need you to assemble the rifle. Quickly now. We don't have much time."

Bill raised his head and looked around slowly, coming to his senses. "Um…okay." His voice cracked and hissed. He struggled and pulled himself to a sitting position by grabbing the fence and a branch on the bush. Then he threw up. He saw some of it was bright red. He knew he was dying.

"William, I need you to focus. Please."

Slowly he reached for the case and fumbled with the latches. Everything that was lighter before was now extremely heavy. He opened the case and began to assemble the rifle. Every movement made him feel like there were sharp rocks in his joints.

"Hey," he said with a raspy voice, "Why didn't you…just have me…kill the Russian?" He was having trouble breathing as well.

"I did think of that, William. But every scenario was extremely complicated. The likelihood of failure was multiplied by many factors. Also, you must know something else I didn't show you. This man you're about to kill is a very good president. He made a speech some time ago about sending a man to the Moon and returning him safely. After today he will become a martyr of sorts to the space program, and they will race with the Soviets to go to the Moon. This will become very important in Earth's future, as space travel will one day save mankind again. If he doesn't die today, that will not happen in time.

"And besides, you're preventing World War Three, William. You saw what will happen in a few months. This president, along with billions of others, will be dead. After Washington was destroyed, a chain reaction was set off. Almost every nuclear weapon in the world was sent to its designated target. Your actions today will stop all that."

Bill could hear a crowd of people nearby. They sounded excited. He had finished assembling the rifle and chambering a round.

"Now, William. You must stand up. His car is approaching, and I must leave you. I feel compelled to move on, and the feeling is very strong. I simply can't fight it any longer. It has been a pleasure working with you, William. I'm happy to say you were the right man for the mission, and I made the correct choice. It's all up to you now. God speed."

"Wait!" Bill said, but he could tell Russell was gone. Just…gone—never to return. A feeling of utter loneliness washed over him.

The crowd was getting louder, and Bill knew time was running out. He summoned all his strength and got to his hands and knees. The pain was incredible. He heard the first shot.

He only managed to stand with the help of the fence and bush and looked over toward the street. The car was already turning the corner. Bill bent and picked up the rifle from where he had leaned it against the fence. Every movement took tremendous effort and he felt like he was trying to fight a strong underwater current.

Just as he managed to put the heavy rifle to his shoulder and look through the scope, he heard the second shot.

The president's hands went to his throat.

He rested the rifle on the fence, between two pickets.

He flicked off the safety, and muscle memory took over.

He closed his eyes, and was able to force himself to stop shaking.

The sounds of the world quieted to a dull murmur. He focused on his one task. He pushed away the pressure riding on this one moment. It was a simple thing really, and he'd done it hundreds of times before. What was one more time?

He opened his eyes.

The crosshairs moved over the president's head.

He pulled the trigger.

Chapter 70

A series of events took place in the split second after Bill pulled the trigger.

The bullet exited the rifle barrel and traveled the short distance to the president's head. A very good man died instantly. One man's life ended so billions could live. A nation would mourn, but the world would survive.

As everyone there watched the leader of their country die, three small stones buried in the ground surrounding the president's car released their energy and turned from pearlescent to a translucent white, transforming from raw opals into ordinary quartz.

A spherical space ship at the bottom of the Gulf of Mexico was there, and then it wasn't.

The recoil of the rifle snapped Bill's clavicle, which was already weakened from the cancer. The pain signal raced toward his brain but never made it there.

And Bill himself, with all his belongings, quietly disappeared because the reality he had just created no longer had a dark future before it. And no one— no one at all, would ever know he had been there.

<u>Epilogue</u>

Russell Bartholomew Jacobson turned off his alarm. He got out of bed and strolled down the hall to answer nature's call. He couldn't believe it was Thursday already. He had labs on Thursdays, and the kids these days were horrible. If they weren't texting during class they were trying to make bombs with the chemicals.

He finished his morning routine and got dressed. He woke Sharon, his wife of thirty-one years, with a soft touch on her back and then a kiss on her mouth.

She said, "I'm sorry, I didn't get up." They were both getting on in years, and she couldn't make him breakfast as often as she used to.

He told her, "That's okay, sweetie. If I didn't have to go to work I'd sleep all day, right here in this bed with you."

She smiled and they kissed again. "Love you, have a good day," she said and closed her eyes.

"Love you too." He stood there for a moment and watched her—loved her. Then he headed for the garage door.

His cell began to ring in his pocket when he got to the living room. He rushed into the garage before answering so he wouldn't wake his wife.

"Hello."

"Mr. Jacobson?"

"Yes, may I ask who is calling?"

"This is Detective Hal Michaels from the Austin Police. It's about your brother."

Russell's hand went to his forehead. "What's he done now?"

"We're holding him in custody on a charge of domestic abuse. He's requested your presence."

"Wait…is Janet okay?"

"She's in the hospital with a bruised up face, but they said her injuries are minor. She'll be fine."

Russell thought for a moment, and then sighed. "I'm sorry, but I can't come in again. I've already missed work twice this year because of him doing the same thing. Please tell him to talk with a lawyer."

"Understood." The detective hung up without saying goodbye.

He considered going in to talk about it with Sharon, but then thought it wasn't worth it. His twin brother had always been in trouble and always would be. It was his nature. Janet should have left him for good long ago, but she always came back for more—no sense in Sharon going to comfort her again. They had tried to talk some sense into both of them and it never did any good. He decided to just let it go and not let it bother him.

He got into his car and backed out of the garage, mentally preparing himself to face a whole class of his own teenaged troublemakers.

* * *

Sheriff Bill Stratton sat in his patrol car in the early morning sun and reveled in the taste of his coffee. He was on a hill overlooking the town where he had grown up, at a spot where the teenagers usually went to make out. He had even visited this place with his own female companions in his youth. It was abandoned at this hour. It was the quietest time of the day, and he liked this shift better than any other: midnight to eight. His small cadre of officers had tried to tell him that it was a rookie slot, but he always replied that they had families too. It was no secret he worked this shift as often as he could. Lots of trouble could happen up until about three, but after that even the criminals were too tired.

His shift almost over. He sent his wife a text telling her he was headed back to the station and would be home soon. It was his oldest granddaughter's birthday today, and she was the ripe old age of four. They were having a party this afternoon, and he had stopped into an all night shopping center and bought her a huge stuffed bear. It was currently sitting strapped into the back seat where criminals usually sat after being arrested.

"Well Mr. Bear," he said to his quiet perpetrator, "It's time to take you in. You've been charged with avoiding my granddaughter and loitering on a store shelf. Your sentence is to be hugged and drooled on while she sleeps with you in her bed, until the stuffing is squeezed completely out of you." He smiled to himself as he started the engine and turned the cruiser around. It was time to go home.